call of the white fox

by **Willis Lindquist**

call of the white fox

illustrated by P. A. HUTCHISON

WHITTLESEY HOUSE, McGRAW-HILL BOOK COMPANY, INC.

NEW YORK   TORONTO   LONDON

to Eric of Maplewood

Library of Congress Catalog Card Number: 56-13396

Published by Whittlesey House
A division of the McGraw-Hill Book Company, Inc.
PRINTED IN THE UNITED STATES OF AMERICA

Also by Willis Lindquist
BURMA BOY

Contents

1- charge of the wolf dog

IT WAS a warm August day. Golden sunlight flooded the tundra—the great treeless plains along the northern coast of Alaska. An uneasy stillness hung over the Eskimo village of Cape North at the edge of the beach. And beyond the broad margin of sand—where Eskimo women were mending their gill nets—tumbled the restless, gray-green waters of the Arctic Ocean.

7

Mark McRoy and his sister Milly came out of their father's trading post and quickly skirted the Eskimo tents where tethered sled dogs sniffed and eyed them with suspicion. They passed the frame schoolhouse, where their mother taught school during the winter, and hurried west across the grassy flat toward the river.

Mark, who was thirteen, and half a head taller than Milly, held his hands against the animal concealed in his red flannel shirt. He glanced back toward the village. Three of Anga's big sled dogs were still watching him.

Milly was bubbling with laughter and chatter as she skipped along beside him, her golden braids and sky-blue sweater flopping with every leap. Mark could understand her happiness. This was the first time he had allowed her to tag along on his secret walks up the river.

Once again he glanced back. This time he caught a glimpse of a familiar Eskimo face above one of the sod Eskimo houses.

"Hey, Oka!" he yelled. "I been looking for you. Come on!"

For a moment Oka stared back. Then, without a word, he ducked out of sight.

"I bet he was hiding from you again," said Milly.

8

Mark was too stunned to say anything. Now Oka wouldn't even talk to him! Oka had been acting strangely for almost a week. In the last four days he had been almost impossible to find. Mark couldn't understand it. That his very best friend, who had been coming with him every day on his secret walks up the river, should suddenly avoid him and stop talking to him made no sense at all.

"If you ask me, there's something mysterious going on," said Milly. "Old Anga dreamed something bad was going to happen. Remember? And no one knows what became of the Eskimos who went out walrus hunting. Maybe some evil spell has come over the village."

Mark did not answer. Milly loved mysteries, and her imagination was as lively as a runaway dog team chasing after a snowshoe rabbit.

"Know what Tani says?" asked Milly. "She says she's almost afraid to be my friend because trading-post people never stay here very long and it's real sad to lose a good friend. Maybe Oka's afraid to be your friend."

"Just because business is poor it doesn't mean we're going to move. Anyway, that's no reason for Oka to be mad at me."

Mark was becoming annoyed with Oka. He al-

9

most wished he were back on his grandfather's farm in Wisconsin, where he and Milly and their mother had lived when his father was stationed in Alaska with the Army.

His father had liked Alaska and believed in its future so much that he had taken all his savings and bought the trading post here at Cape North. For over a year he had run the trading post all by himself until he had saved up enough money to send for his family.

Mark remembered how thrilled he and Milly and his mother had been about coming way up here to the Arctic, the last great frontier in America, as his father had called it. But now they had been here two whole years, and Mark still had the feeling that he was an outsider in the Eskimo village.

It wasn't that he didn't like the Eskimos. He did. They were always kind and polite and friendly. And yet, he never quite felt that he really knew them. They had so many secrets they wanted to keep from him. Oka had been his first really close friend. They had been constantly together during the summer, and now, for some mysterious reason, Oka had suddenly turned against him.

Mark was still so upset as they neared the river that he completely forgot about the big sled dogs

10

in the village. He opened his shirt. Out popped a black-button nose, followed by a blue-gray head with bright round eyes and stand-up ears. The arctic fox cub was not much over two months old. Its blue-gray fur felt as soft and fluffy as new-fallen snow. The instant Kali's paws touched the earth he was off in a flash to the end of his rawhide leash.

The sled dogs in the village suddenly began howling. Mark glanced back in dismay. They had seen the fox cub and were leaping against their chains. He saw Anga, Oka's grandfather, rush from his summer tent with his rifle. Women and children came running from their fish nets on the beach.

Mark dashed for the river, with Kali racing ahead and Milly following. They did not pause till they had dropped out of sight below the cut of the river.

Milly giggled. "Didn't Anga look funny coming out with his gun?"

Mark bit his lip. His carelessness had disturbed the whole village. He did not find anything funny about Anga coming out with his rifle. Hunting had been very poor during the summer, and Anga probably thought the dogs were howling at some wild animal. The women, too, had been disappointed, for they must have hoped that someone was coming with word of their husbands, the missing walrus hunters. He knew his mother and father were going to scold him for letting the dogs see Kali.

"Just my luck," he muttered. "I wanted to prove to Dad and Mom that Kali wasn't any trouble to anybody, so they'd like him and let me keep him."

"Mom says it's a sin keeping a wild thing in the house," said Milly. She stooped to pet Kali, who was busily digging under a flat stone. "You never could have kept him at all if he hadn't been an orphan and too young to take care of himself."

Mark knew that very well. It had been six weeks since he and Oka had rescued the starving cub from an attacking owl near the den where the mother fox had been shot by a trigger-happy tourist. "Kali's not wild any more. I've been training him real good."

Kali continued digging under the rock.

"There must be something under that rock," said Mark, shoving it aside with his foot.

Kali pounced on the uncovered spot, his front feet churning. Sand flew. He soon uncovered three duck eggs and a half-grown loon in pinfeathers.

12

Mark was not surprised, for he had often watched wild foxes dig holes to store food for the winter. He allowed Kali to have one of the eggs and covered the others again, then moved the stone back in place.

As they walked along the sandy edge of the lazy Sitkin River, Mark ordered the cub to heel. Kali trotted along beside him, glancing up now and then as if to ask, "Am I doing all right?"

Mark almost burst with pride. "See, Milly? He heeled perfect for thirty steps. That's a new record. He's still too young to keep his mind on anything for long."

"Can you make him sit?"

"Not yet." He forced the cub to sit and took off its leash. "Now stay there. Stay!"

Kali reached out and licked the finger Mark was wagging in front of his nose. It struck Milly so funny she burst out laughing.

"Stay!" Mark ordered. He got up and walked away, motioning for Milly to follow.

"But, Mark! Won't he run away?"

Mark grinned. She still thought of Kali as a wild animal, but she'd soon change her mind. "Don't worry. Oka and I trained him like this every day."

When he had gone about a hundred feet he

turned and whistled. Kali came scooting, and yipped and danced about them until Mark picked him up and fed him a bit of dried meat. That was what he wanted. He nuzzled Mark's neck and gave him a lick under the chin.

Milly laughed and clapped her hands. "He's twice as fast as a puppy."

"Only one thing on the tundra can run faster than a fox, and that's a snowshoe rabbit."

"Tani says a fox can catch a rabbit."

"Sure it can. By hiding near a rabbit trail. When a rabbit comes hopping along the fox gets it in one jump." Mark put the cub down. "Kali likes to box. Watch this."

He struck out with his open hand. Kali met it with his front paws. Again and again Mark tried to hit the cub, but the paws were always faster. Kali danced in and out, yipping excitedly, for this was a game he dearly loved.

"Why don't you play with him like this at home?" asked Milly.

" 'Cause he always yips when he gets excited, and that makes Mom mad."

"Mom and Dad would like him if they saw the cute things he can do. They don't know you've

14

been training him. Do you have to keep it a secret?"

"That's part of my plan," said Mark. "Next Sunday I'm going to take Dad out here and surprise him. When he sees what Kali can do he'll let me keep him."

Milly's blue eyes sparkled. "Oh, Mark, if it only works!"

Mark fastened the rawhide leash to the cub's sealskin collar again. "His blue-gray color makes him look kind of dirty now, but this winter he'll turn pure white, just like the snowshoe rabbits do. I guess I'll be the only one in the world with a white arctic fox for a pet!"

Having an arctic fox of his very own still filled him with a sense of wonder. It was almost too good to be true. He wanted to tell Milly how Kali slept under his chin at night—a warm, soft ball of fur against his neck, making him feel he could never, never be lonely again. But he doubted that Milly would understand.

Several sandpipers flew up as they continued on up the river. Once a white-fronted goose rose from the water, leaving a silvery trail of ripples near the far bank of the river.

They gathered willow leaves so their mother could make an Eskimo green salad. The steep banks of the river were covered with willows. The trunks and branches grew like vines along the ground, for here in the far North, three hundred miles above the Arctic Circle, very few things ever grew to be more than six inches high.

For a short while they went wading so that Milly could see how Kali could swim. And then, as eve-

16

ning shadows lengthened, and the birds were on wing again, they headed slowly back for the village.

Kali suddenly dived into the willow brush and backed out holding a bird in his mouth.

With a cry Milly grabbed it. "A snow bunting," she wailed. "And Kali broke its wing!"

Mark looked at it helplessly.

"Let's take it to Anga," said Milly. "Anga can fix anything." She started off, cupping the bird in her hands.

For a time they walked swiftly. Then suddenly they heard the howling of village dogs. They stopped short and looked at each other.

"Did you hear that?" said Milly. "People are shouting, too!"

"I'll bet the walrus hunters are back!" cried Mark. "Come on!"

Up the slope he went, scrambling through thickets of ground willow and over rocks at a pace that was almost too much for the little fox.

As he reached the tundra the village came into sight—the red and white trading post and the schoolhouse, the grass-covered mounds which were the Eskimos' winter homes, and, closer to the sea, the canvas tents where the Eskimos lived in the

17

summer.   Beyond all this Mark saw a large skin boat and a crowd on the beach.   Everyone in the village seemed to be there.

"It's them!" he shouted.   "See the boat?   And there's Jocko."

Even at that distance it was easy to recognize Jocko, the big Husky that Pack Ice Charlie had taken along on the hunt.   The dog was larger and more wolflike than the other sled dogs.

They had to cross a swampy place over springy humps of cotton grass.   But as they came closer, Mark could hear the voices and laughter above the howling of the chained dogs.   The noise frightened Kali, and he hung back at the end of his leash.

"Know what this means, Milly?" Mark asked. "An all-night celebration!"

"There'll be a big feast, and maybe a drum dance, too."

Mark could see his young Eskimo friends Oka and Luke and Joe coming up the beach with a heavy bundle of skins.   He yelled to them.

Oka saw him and became strangely excited.   He dropped his side of the bundle and waved with both arms, as though he wanted them to go away.

Mark frowned, remembering the strange way Oka had turned against him.   Now the other boys

18

were making go-away signals. They shouted something that sounded like a warning, and kept glancing back toward the boat.

Mark followed their glances. Suddenly he saw, and understood. Bounding up the beach came the giant dog Jocko. Somehow, in the excitement, the Husky had broken loose. It was free!

Mark knew what would happen if it spotted his pet fox. Turning quickly, he caught up the cub. With trembling fingers he tore at his shirt buttons. If only he could hide Kali inside his shirt before. . . .

A choked cry broke from Milly.

Even before he shot a glance over his shoulder he knew Jocko had seen Kali. Jocko was coming. He was streaking right for them in mighty leaps, as savage and deadly in attack as a white arctic wolf.

2- Kali disappears

MARK RAN.

Jocko, Pack Ice Charlie's best polar-bear hunting dog, was not the kind of dog you could frighten off with shouts and arm waving. It feared nothing. Once it had chased a polar bear for miles across broken ice, nipping at its heels, delaying it time and again, until the hunters came up with their rifles.

Mark knew he had small chance of saving his cub from Jocko's powerful jaws. He knew Jocko would tear him to pieces, if need be, to get at the cub. But he ran as he never had run before, with Kali in his arms, and his long-legged shadow racing beside him with giant steps.

There was no place to go. Ahead, stretching out as flat as the sea to the far horizon, lay the brown arctic tundra. It had no protection to offer, no shelter, no tree to climb.

The race was a hopeless one. It could last only seconds more. Though Kali was doomed, Mark kept running at top speed. Sharp pains stabbed at his side. Out of the corner of his eye he saw another shadow closing swiftly behind his own.

Milly's shrill warning came from a distance. "He'll jump you, Mark! Drop Kali! Let him go!"

Let Kali go! It was the one thing he could not do. The fox cub loved and trusted him. It looked to him for protection. He could not fail it now, not without a fight.

The wolf dog's shadow came in with a rush. Mark saw it spring for the kill, straight at his own shadow.

He spun. He tried to duck.

He saw a gray blur and a flash of fangs. The snarling wolf dog struck him full in the chest. He was knocked off his feet. Kali flew from his arms, squealing in terror.

Mark tried to hold on to the wolf dog as it struggled to get to its feet. His clawing fingers hooked the dog's collar—not a moment too soon. His arm

22

was almost jerked from its socket as the beast found its legs and lunged after the fleeing cub.

Mark hung on. He was dragged and jolted over the ground. Weeds whipped his face. He knew the enraged wolf dog might turn on him in an instant and fight its way free with slashing fangs.

But the life of his pet was all that mattered. Unless he could hold on, Kali would die. With a desperate effort he threw his free arm over the dog's back, caught a firm grip on the heavy fur, and gave a mighty tug.

The wolf dog tripped and came down on top of him. They rolled. Before the dog could break away Mark had his legs around the small of its back in a tight scissor hold.

The big Husky twisted and squirmed and snarled with rage. Mark got his arms about the shaggy neck and hung on desperately.

In the distance, he could hear Milly's screams for help. He felt weak and trembly. There was a pain in his leg he had not noticed before.

After a time he saw Milly running past at a safe distance. "It's all right, Mark," she cried. "They're coming to help. I'll go get Kali."

He had no breath to answer her. But he smiled to himself. Jocko could not get away. Kali was safe. Soon Milly would find him and bring him back.

Eskimos came running up. Pack Ice Charlie grabbed his dog and drew it away.

"Brave boy, Mark," he said. "You many brave like a hunter."

It was the finest compliment an Eskimo could give, and it came from the most fearless hunter in the village. The other Eskimos smiled and nodded, all except his friend Oka, who looked frightened.

Timidly Oka helped him to his feet. "You hurt, Mark?" he asked.

Mark shook his head. The front of his red shirt was torn. He was bruised and scratched, and his left leg hurt when he walked. But he had lived with Eskimos long enough to know that men of the Arctic suffered their pains in silence.

He said, "I better go help Milly find Kali."

He hoped Oka would offer to come along. But Oka didn't. He seemed uneasy and glanced toward the village as if anxious to get back to the beach.

Mark hurried away to hide his disappointment. Oka was acting more and more like a stranger. Why? Why? What was wrong with him?

Mark had not gone very far, limping to favor his

bruised leg, when Milly came up from the river. She did not have the fox cub. In spite of his sore leg he ran to meet her.

"Where's Kali? Didn't you—"

Big silvery tears rolled down Milly's cheeks. "I —I don't know." She choked back a sob. "I looked. I called. I hunted everywhere. He's gone, Mark. What can we do?" She covered her face with her hands and started to cry.

Kali gone? It couldn't be true.

"He's been scared near out of his skin," Mark said. "He's hiding somewhere, that's all. You sure he went down to the river?"

She nodded, wiping her tears with the back of a hand.

"Then he's down there in the willows." He led the way down. Blue shadows cast a gloom over the river and gave the air a chill that made him shiver.

"Here, Kali! Here, Kali!"

How still it seemed. It was as though the whole world waited and listened with him. Out of lonely space, far off to the left, came the high quivering wail of a loon—a sound so filled with sorrow the Eskimos spoke of it as the cry of a lost spirit. Mark was touched by its sadness as never before.

With Milly's help he searched the leafy bank in both directions. A snowshoe rabbit broke from cover a few yards ahead and in two leaps disappeared over the rim of the tundra. Lemmings, the tundra mice which looked like tiny guinea pigs, made rustling sounds in the brush as they scurried away. But Kali was nowhere in sight.

Again and again Mark called. His voice grew shrill, for a tightness had come into his throat. Milly began to cry again.

"We just have to keep looking," he told her.

There would be light enough to search all night, if necessary. When the sun dipped below the northern horizon about eleven o'clock, there would be two hours of silvery twilight and then the pink dawn of another day.

It was a good thing Oka had not come along, Mark decided. Oka would have given up after the first few minutes, convinced that Kali had run away.

For some reason none of the Eskimos understood how he felt about Kali. They all seemed to think a fox couldn't be tamed. They believed that Kali belonged to some strange and invisible thing called the spirit of wild foxes. They said the voice of the spirit came to him on the wind—calling, calling,

26

always calling him back to run with his kind on the tundra.

But Mark knew they were wrong. Kali was not like other foxes. He was a tame house fox who lived with people. He had been lapping condensed milk out of a soup bowl most of his life.

No, Kali wasn't wild, and he wouldn't think of running away. Yet the tundra seemed to have swallowed him up.

Milly gave a shout. She was on her hands and knees at the edge of the river, and she seemed excited. He limped down to her as fast as he could.

"I think I found his tracks," she said.

The tracks in the sand were those of a young fox. They were fresh, even fresher than the tracks Kali had made along the beach an hour ago, and they went right across the sand and into the water.

"He crossed the river!" Mark exclaimed. "Now we know where to look."

"We can't get across without a boat."

"We'll go home and get Anga's kayak," he said. "Come on."

It was a long half mile to the village. Every now and then Milly stopped to peek at the wounded snow bunting, which was now in her sweater pocket. Milly looked so tired and cold he felt sorry for her. He was suddenly afraid she might give up when they reached home. If she did, he would have to face the big, smothering loneliness of the tundra all by himself. He did not want that to happen.

"We'll get our jackets and have something to eat before we get the kayak," he said. "It won't take long to find Kali."

His limp was becoming worse. The muscles in his leg had twisted into a hard knot that grew tighter and more painful with every step.

As they entered the village the sunset sky was

28

aflame, sweeping the earth with tints of rose and yellow. The canvas tents were a brilliant orange against the darkening sea. Warm smells of cooking and of driftwood fires hung in the still evening air, and the babble of voices and laughter floated up from the beach.

They were surprised to find their mother waiting for them at home. The chill in her blue eyes was like a tapping foot—her strict teacher look.

She seemed to know what had happened, for she asked no questions. She took a look at Mark's scratched chest and made him lie down on his bunk. Not until she had bathed and dressed his wounds did Mark have a chance to explain that he had to get the kayak so he could find Kali.

"You're like ice," she said. "You lie there while I heat some soup for you and Milly."

When the soup was ready Milly finished hers in a few moments and hurried out. Mark was trying to get up courage to follow her when his mother came in with a bottle of green liniment and began rubbing his leg. "You've probably sprained it," she said. "I'll have your father come in and look at it later."

"But Kali—"

Her eyes softened. "No, dear. You're in no

condition to look for Kali now. I'm sorry. It's probably best to leave things just as they are. A fox has no place in the house. We couldn't have kept him through the winter."

What was she saying? It took him a moment to get his breath. "But, Mom! Don't you understand? Kali's lost! He's out there on the tundra all alone. He's afraid. He's hungry. He's looking for me this very minute!"

"I know." She rubbed his leg more gently. "Kali was a sweet pet, even though he did chew up our furs and was always underfoot. I loved him, too. But now we've done all we can for him. He's old enough to take care of himself."

Mark stared at her. How could she say she loved Kali and then turn against him when he was lost and needed help?

"You mean I can't go after Kali and bring him back—not—not ever?"

3- a mysterious boat

"SUPPOSE we let your father decide," said his mother. She capped the bottle of liniment and went out through the front room, which was the trading post.

Mark heard sounds of Eskimos on the beach,

31

where the meat was being cut up and divided among the families. He lay in his bunk for a long time without stirring. He knew what his father would say. Kali would never be allowed in the house again. Mark felt tired and helpless—and so empty inside he could not cry.

He could hear Eskimo children coming and going. They would be gathering driftwood along the beach. The Eskimo cookstoves, made out of oil drums, would take a lot of wood; for the stewing and baking would continue through most of the night.

The lively yelping of dogs told him when people were passing with loads of meat. Most of the meat would be stored in deep holes in the frozen earth, the Eskimo ice cellars, where it would freeze and remain fresh till needed.

Milly came in with the snow bunting. Anga had set its broken wing and bound it in place with a soft leather thong.

She had forgotten all about Kali. Her eyes danced as she told of her plans for the long night of celebration. She and her Eskimo friends, Tani and Helen and Doris, were going to eat and eat and eat, and then play records over in Tani's tent. While

32

listening to music they would look over the new mail-order catalogue Texas Andy, the bush pilot, had brought, and pick out things they would like for Christmas. They would watch the drum dance, if there was one, and listen to the story-telling.

"Something terrible happened on the hunt," she went on, hardly pausing for breath. "Tani wasn't going to tell at first. Eskimos aren't supposed to tell white people about curses and things. White people always laugh."

"Did she tell?"

Milly nodded. "The boat turned over and Pack Ice Charlie lost his raven feathers and wolf skull and his carved ivory seal, the best lucky charms he ever had. The hunters didn't have any luck after that. They think it's a bad sign, and a bad sign is like a curse. Bad things are sure to happen."

Mark was almost glad when she left. He turned up the flame in the lamp by his bunk. He didn't believe in curses, but the creepy way Milly spoke about them made him feel uneasy. The north country had enough mysteries without her help. There was even a mystery about the Sitkin River. Eskimos never went on the other side. It was almost as if they believed that the tundra beyond was a place of hidden dangers. Yet, they refused to answer questions about it. Why?

Mark became restless and tried to get up. Sharp pains stabbed at his leg and side. He fell back with a gasp. His muscles had stiffened. Now he was not even going to be able to hear the stories of the hunt.

Loneliness closed over him. Kali was gone. Had Oka still been his friend he would have been right there, sitting on the edge of the bunk, trying to cheer him up. But Oka was not there. He wasn't coming.

Sadly Mark watched the sunset fade from the little square window and took a deep, deep breath. It was hard to believe that Oka had turned against him. They had been having so much fun together. They had even shared a few secrets, like training the fox, and having secret meeting places on the tundra. When Oka was with him the Eskimo village seemed almost like home. But now suddenly he was lonely again, like a visitor in a village of friendly strangers.

All at once his father was beside his bunk, standing tall and lean in the lamplight. His dark eyes seemed to smile as he held out a driftwood platter of boiled seal meat. There were hunks of blubber and liver on one side, and on the other some brown bread freshly baked by Tani's mother.

"We can't have you missing the feast, son," said his father cheerfully.

"Dad, I—"

"We can talk about Kali later." His father sat on the edge of the bunk and, holding the platter in his lap, gave Mark a slow wink. "A man needs food when he's got problems. Helps him to think."

Though not hungry, Mark wanted to please his father. Slowly he rose on one elbow. They ate Eskimo style, picking up pieces of meat with their fingers. They grinned at each other because Mark's mother wasn't there to see that they ate properly.

His father's unusual cheerfulness made Mark curious, for he knew how worried his father was about poor business at his trading post.

"Dad, you seem so pleased. Did the Eskimos bring back lots of ivory to trade?"

"No. It was another poor hunt. There isn't even going to be a drum dance. If hunting doesn't soon get better I don't know what's going to happen to my business."

Mark could understand that. When hunting was poor the Eskimos had no furs to trade for things

35

they needed at the post. Then business was bad.

Mark said, "I guess you acted cheerful just to cheer me up so I wouldn't feel so bad about Kali."

"Partly that. But I have good reason for being pleased. I saw how you fought Jocko to save your fox cub." Again a smile lighted his face and he leaned over and pushed his fist gently against Mark's chin. "You may not be much of a hunter yet, but you'll learn. It takes the kind of courage you showed today. This is a hard, tough country, Mark; and we have to be strong to live in it."

"Yes, sir," Mark said, almost in a whisper. But he knew he hadn't been brave at all. He had been frightened half to death when the dog leaped at him. Deep in his heart he knew he could never be as strong and brave as the Eskimo boys. Nothing could frighten them.

"As for Kali," said his father, "the time has come when he should have his freedom. The house would be too warm for him this winter."

"Couldn't I keep him outside on a chain?"

"He wouldn't be happy. On a chain he'd probably become as ill-tempered as most of those dogs out there. He needs his freedom now so he can learn to hunt for his food. If he doesn't learn to hunt before winter comes he'll starve."

36

"But Kali is still dragging his leash. What if it gets tangled up in the willows?"

"It was a rawhide leash. Kali would nip it in two if it got caught."

The last flicker of hope died in Mark's heart. He wiped his hands on the wet towel his father brought and sank back on his bunk.

His father studied him for a moment. "Is there some trouble between you and Oka? He was sitting out there on the step when I came. He slipped away as soon as he saw me."

"Oka? Sitting on *our* step?"

"Yes, and I've never seen him looking quite so unhappy."

Mark swallowed hard. Oka had not forgotten about him. Oka was unhappy, too. "I guess he feels sorry because he wouldn't talk to me this afternoon. Dad, if you see him please tell him to come. Tell him I'm not mad."

Mark's sore muscles kept him in the house for two days. They were two long, endless days. Oka did not come to see him. The kitchen and bunkroom seemed strangely silent without Kali bouncing around, yipping for attention.

Sometimes Mark heard the lonely cry of a fox

cub in the distance, and he knew that Kali was out there beyond the river, hungry and calling to him for food.

On the third day, while he was having breakfast, Milly and Tani came rushing in breathlessly to tell him they had just seen Kali beyond the river. Mark grabbed his leather jacket and his father's binoculars and hurried out the back door of the long one-story trading-post building.

He passed between the sod Eskimo houses. They stood empty now. They were too dark and damp for use during the summer months.

His leg bothered him hardly at all as he broke into a trot across the tundra. He made for the big bend in the Sitkin where Milly and Tani had been picking berries when they saw Kali. At least fifteen minutes had passed since then. Would Kali still be there?

Just before reaching the river he dropped down and crawled the last few yards. His hands trembled as he raised the glasses to his eyes. Just to see his pet once again, to watch it from a distance without being seen, that was all he wanted.

He searched in vain for several minutes. The sudden stirring of willow leaves on the far bank made him hold his breath. Presently three plump ptarmigan, arctic grouse which the Eskimos called "tundra chickens," broke from cover to peck at something near the edge of the river.

Farther along the bank a rusty-brown eider duck hen stood calmly preening her feathers in a clump of cotton grass. She would not have been nearly so bold, he knew, if a young fox had been near.

Mark turned to study the upstream bend of the river. There was no sign of life. But just at the bend, above the tea-brown swirl of the lazy river, he discovered a strange lump in a thicket of willows. It did not move. It was too large to be any kind of an animal. Somehow it seemed out of place.

Puzzled, Mark rose and walked toward it for a closer look. As he approached the bend he suddenly stopped short and stared in amazement. It was a skin boat, the most unusual boat he had ever seen. Crudely made and ugly in shape, it had a wide, flat bottom. None of the village Eskimos would ever make such a clumsy craft. What puzzled him most was that the strange boat had been landed on the other side of the river, where none of the Eskimos liked to go. There was nothing over there but swamps and empty tundra.

Everything about the boat seemed mysterious and unfriendly, and somehow frightening.

4- Mark goes hunting

AS MARK stood looking at the strange boat he heard a sound that made him turn. Oka was coming up with a .22 rifle over his shoulder.

Oka smiled shyly. "You go hunting with me, Mark?"

Mark stared at the Eskimo boy. He found his tongue at last. "L-l-look over there . . . across the river . . . that boat. . . ."

When Oka spotted the boat his eyes widened. "You see who put it there?" he whispered.

41

"No." Now Mark was whispering, too. "Did you see that kind before?"

Shaking his head, Oka searched the tundra beyond for several moments.

Mark said, "Whoever built it must have made it for the river. The sides aren't high enough to keep out ocean waves."

"And they tried to hide it so no one could find, but the wind took off the branches," said Oka, glancing about on all sides. "We better go fast away before anyone find us looking."

As they hurried off Mark said, "Any honest person coming down the river would have gone right to the village."

They walked swiftly for several minutes. Mark suddenly realized they were going upstream, away from the village. "Hey! This isn't the way home."

"We go to the goose marshes where hunting is good."

Mark stopped. Hunting was the last thing he wanted to do. "I didn't say I was going hunting."

A hurt look came into Oka's face. "You mad with me, Mark?"

"Well,—" Mark began uncertainly. He was ashamed to admit that the thought of killing anything gave him a sick, wiggly feeling in his stomach.

"Mark, I didn't go with you and Kali up the river any more because the boys were laughing at me." Oka hung his head. "My grandfather Anga said it was right for them to laugh. He said it was foolish for a big boy to spend so much time with a pet. Pets are only for small children, toys to play with."

Mark felt his face growing hot. He had not realized before how Eskimos felt about pets. They thought of their dogs as useful work animals, nothing more. "If they laughed at you they must have been laughing at me, too."

Oka wrinkled his nose, an Eskimo way of saying "no." "You are different. You are from the States."

"You always say that," complained Mark. "I don't want to be different. I want to be like everybody else."

Oka's smile suddenly returned. "Now Kali is gone and we don't have to worry. No one can laugh now. We can go hunting. We can bring home meat and show everybody we can work like the men."

Mark glanced longingly at the village. He had hoped to get the boys to play ball that afternoon. He liked baseball. It was the one thing he could do better than any of the Eskimo boys. But now he was ashamed to mention the game. And he was happy to be with Oka again. He had to please Oka.

"Well, all right," he said. "I'll go along to keep you company."

Oka smiled cheerfully. "Your mother said if we bring home a goose she will make the big, big dinner, like a Christmas feast."

Just thinking about a fat goose roasted to a golden brown, and smelling of sage dressing, was enough to make Mark's mouth water.

Finding a goose would be easy. Game birds were everywhere. Above, hundreds of geese and ducks were winging across the sky. And all about on the tundra the swamps and reedy margins were alive with feathery flutterings and the flapping of wings.

Oka selected a quiet marsh near the river. It was deserted, but feathers and nests of white-fronted geese covered the ground. "The geese soon come back, I think," said Oka.

Mark had nothing to say. Oka knew more about geese than he did, for Oka had been hunting them with a rifle for several years.

"You shoot first," said Oka, offering his .22.

"No, you—"

But Oka forced the rifle into his hands. "Get down. I cover you good."

Lying a few yards from the water, Mark allowed himself to be covered with grass and short tundra brush. Then Oka went off to hide below the cut of the river. Mark wasn't at all sure he'd have nerve enough to press the trigger. If he couldn't get off a shot when the big birds came down, Oka would know how he felt about killing things. Soon everyone in the village would know his weakness, and even his own father would have to be ashamed of him.

Presently he heard whisperings in the air, then a great stirring above him. A large flock of geese came sweeping down, legs forward, their powerful wings ripping the air with loud, whooshing sounds.

There were so many together he did not need to take aim. He closed his eyes and squeezed the trigger. He shot again as the geese, honking and flapping in alarm, rose into the air.

With a shudder he got to his feet, not daring to look toward the water. If he had hit anything he did not want to see it, not right away.

"You got one!" shouted Oka, running up on short, powerful legs.

Half an hour later Oka shot three from a blind. He had waded out and brought in two of them by the time Mark came from his hiding place. The third, a large gander, floated in deep water beyond Oka's reach. How they were going to get it Mark could not imagine. It made him feel stupid and helpless, for he knew the problem would seem very simple to a skillful hunter like Oka.

Unwinding a long leather thong from his waist Oka tied one end to a stone, then cast the stone so that it fell just beyond the floating bird. The leather thong caught in the gander's open wing. With gentle tugs the boy drew the goose slowly ashore.

Oka grinned. "I shoot three because my hunting charm bring me good luck." He drew out the small leather charm bag which hung at his throat and showed Mark an ancient ivory carving of a seal. "This the most powerful hunting charm in the village. It belong to my grandfather, Anga. In the long ago, when our tribe was called the Seal People, all the hunters have carvings of seal like this one."

On the way home Oka told of a time when the geese came north too early in the spring. All their ponds on the tundra were still frozen. But the sun had melted the top of the ice in places to form pools of meltwater an inch or two deep. The geese had all crowded into these pools to spend the night, for they liked to sleep in water whenever it was possible.

The water froze about their feet while they slept, and several hundred geese found themselves trapped in the new ice. Their honking and flapping could be heard far across the tundra.

Foxes came to feed on them. Snowy owls glided back and forth overhead, waiting for the frantic geese to wear themselves out and become too weak to defend themselves.

When Anga discovered them he sent Oka running back to the village with word that everybody should come. It was very plain, Anga had said, that the spirits of the tundra had kindly trapped the geese for a hungry people, and the spirits would not be well pleased unless everyone shared in the harvest.

Oka's dark eyes flashed as he told the story. "We put many geese in the ice cellars that day," he said.

It was good to be out on the tundra again with Oka. Mark suddenly wanted to please him, and he knew just how to do it.

"Remember what you said about us making a winter camp somewhere up the river?" he asked. "Well, why don't we do it?"

47

Oka looked surprised. "But you said you didn't—"

"I changed my mind. It would be fun having a snowhouse and cooking our own grub. We could go up Fridays after school and come back Saturday nights."

Oka laughed with delight. "My grandfather let me use his camping stove and caribou skins and grub box."

"We can get a lantern and food from the trading post."

As they went on making plans for their winter camp they neared the bend in the river where the mysterious boat lay hidden in the willows. Oka turned away from the river. "We don't go close to that boat this time," he said.

"You scared, Oka?"

The young Eskimo grinned. "My grandfather says the only thing to fear is a bad memory. A bad memory makes you forget to be careful, and when you are not careful you are always in danger."

"But where do you think the boat came from?" asked Mark. "Texas Andy says the river starts up in the Brooks Mountains and comes north three hundred miles through flat tundra where nobody lives."

48

"In the mountains there are people." Oka's face suddenly darkened. "We better tell the men. Maybe—maybe they have seen a boat like this before."

There was a hint of mystery in Oka's voice. Mark cast a glance back over his shoulder and walked a little faster. It seemed to him that Oka knew more about the boat than he cared to tell, and Oka looked worried.

5- Texas Andy calls

FOR A WEEK the village of Cape North lay under a heavy blanket of fog. Then the weather cleared, and once again United States Navy jets were flying their daily patrols along the coast. Three of them thundered past the village, leaving silvery trails in the blue.

50

Mark hardly gave them a glance. He was watching the red plane of the bush pilot coming in from the south. The red plane circled and came down in a smooth glide to land on the beach. Milly and Mark raced after it and reached it before Texas Andy could unwind his long legs and get out of the cabin.

"Any mail for me?" yelled Milly.

"Sure thing!" Texas Andy's face, as usual, was all smiles and squints, and his red hair stood out in all directions like a roaring brush fire. "Here's a letter from your grandma in Wisconsin." The lean pilot stuck his head out and squinted up the beach where the tents had been. "Thunderation! Where is everybody? What happened to the tents?"

"Gone. The Eskimos left about a week ago," replied Mark.

"The most awful thing happened," gasped Milly. "You wouldn't believe it." She was just taking a deep breath to explain when her father came up.

"Tex," he said, shaking hands warmly. "We began to think you'd forgotten us. You haven't been up here since June."

"Been that long? Yep, I reckon so. That last

trip was just before I went down to Fairbanks and got me a helicopter. Man oh man, that thing is fun; like sitting in an egg basket tied to a cloud."

"What's a helicopter?" asked Milly.

"One of them flying egg-beater things. I been using it down south in the tree country, and up and down the Yukon most of the summer."

That part of central Alaska, Mark knew, was where Indian tribes lived, and white men trapped and panned the streams for gold. "Were you flying trappers back to their cabins?" he asked.

"Not so many trappers. It's them tourists and fishermen I been flying into the back country. They come all the way up from the States and want to get back in the mountains and tight little valleys where regular planes can't land. That's how come us bush pilots have to have helicopters now. Hauling tourists is the best-paying business we got."

"Speaking of tourists," said Mark's father, "I hope you don't bring us any more like that last fellow you brought. He was trigger-happy. He shot at every bird and animal he saw, just for kicks."

"He even killed a mother fox," Mark said. "And the snowy owls would have got all the cubs, but I came just in time to save one of them."

52

"Well, I'll be a crow-bait mule if that don't beat all," Texas Andy said angrily. "Some of them tourist hunters is plumb loco. One wanted me to take him out to the ice fields so he could shoot polar bear from the helicopter. Ever hear of such a thing? 'Course he knew I'd been up there looking for bear myself."

Mark's father looked shocked. "You hunted bear with a helicopter?"

"Couple of weeks ago, but not with a gun," Texas Andy replied. He cast a squinty glance at the ice fields—a brilliant white line at the horizon of the sea, with a shimmering halo of light along the edge of the sky above it. "Me and Ben set up a supply base out there on the ice and flew around looking for bear cubs for the zoo in Seattle."

"Did you find any?" Milly wanted to know.

"Took us three days before we spotted a bear and two cubs. She lit out for a big open lead and dived under with her cubs. All we had to do was sit up there in the sky till they come up for air. Then I dropped a loop on the young ones and hauled 'em up one by one, easy as roping steers in a sand pit."

"Did you really?" asked Milly.

Texas Andy showed her the back of his right

hand. "See them scratches? Bear cubs did that. And say, didn't you start to tell me where all the Eskimos went?"

"That's a long story," said Mr. McRoy. "Let's get the mail up to the house. Helen put on coffee the minute she heard your plane."

The bush pilot began digging through bags in the rear of his cabin. He held up a small paper bag. "This is the piece Pack Ice Charlie needs for fixing his rifle. And here's two lengths of stovepipe for Daniel." He tossed the pipes to Mark's father. "This lipstick is for Joe-Joe Henry's daughter, only she don't want nobody to know. Give it to her when there ain't nobody around."

He dug into another mail sack. "Old Mary gave me some red thread and told me to get some cloth to match. You tell her I'm plumb sorry I couldn't find the right shade. Oh yes, and this here is phonograph needles for Tani. That's about all, I reckon, except for the papers and letters."

Mark took the letters. It was his job to box the Eskimo mail at the trading post. Most of the letters were from young Eskimos who had left home to work for the salmon-canning companies in southern Alaska.

Mark's mother met them at the kitchen door.

"You're in luck this time, Tex," she greeted him. "I've just finished a batch of doughnuts. If you'll stay for dinner—"

"I'm mighty obliged, Helen, but I couldn't. I have to get over to Barrow with some special medicine for the hospital."

For Mark it was always a thrill to have Texas Andy stay even for a few minutes. He was their only contact with the outside world, except for the supply ship which brought the heavy supplies, and that came only once each summer.

The tall pilot was dunking his second doughnut before Mark finally had a chance to tell about the mysterious boat he had found in the willows.

"That same night," he went on, "the Eskimos found four more boats like it farther up the river. By morning their tents were down. They had packsacks on most of the dogs and were ready to leave. Anga invited us to go along."

His father said, "When I tried to find out what it was all about, Anga told me we would be in no danger if we wished to stay. I knew I could trust Anga's judgment. I wanted Helen and the children to go along, but they wouldn't leave me here alone."

"Well, if that don't beat all," said Texas Andy. "And now's the time when the Eskimos ought to be

55

out hunting caribou," he added, speaking of the big tundra deer. "If they don't lay in a good store of caribou meat now, what they going to eat this winter?"

"Fish," answered Mark. "They all went to their regular fishing camps up the coast. But they don't usually go until after the first hard freeze when they can use sleds."

"That's right," said his father. "There must be some old Eskimo superstition behind it all. They won't speak to us about their superstitions, you know. But Anga did tell me they were not going caribou hunting this year because there were no caribou to hunt. He said whenever the strange boats come down the river the caribou hunters were always sure to have bad luck. He said that was why they had to leave early for their fishing camps."

"I simply don't understand it," said Mark's mother. "It's been a bad year for everyone with hunting as poor as it is. Our trading-post business hasn't been doing well at all. And now all our customers will be gone for weeks."

"If there had been any real danger," said Mark's father, "I would have had to leave everything. That would have ruined me. I've got cases and cases of canned goods that would have frozen and become worthless if I wasn't here to keep the place heated."

Mark said, "I don't see how a few boats coming down the river could frighten all the caribou away."

"If you ask me," Milly said in her creepiest voice, "those boats brought an evil curse. I read a story once—"

"Milly!" her mother broke in sharply. "Let's hear what Tex has to say."

The bush pilot finished his fourth doughnut. "If there ain't no caribou I figure the Eskimos did right to get to their fishing camps early. They're going to need all the fish they can catch."

"That may be," said Mark's mother, "but I can't help feeling the Eskimos were frightened by those strange boats. This time they wouldn't leave their children here for the opening of school. Even the old ones went along."

Texas Andy ran a hand through his wild red hair. "You folks sure picked yourself the most out-of-the-way place on the Arctic Coast. Always been strange doings around here nobody could understand. I reckon that's why trading-post people never stick it out here very long."

"There can't be any real danger," said Mark's father. He lighted his pipe and gave Milly the

57

match to throw in the coal bucket. "But I would like to know what's behind it all. If you could find out anything—"

"I'll do some asking around," promised Texas Andy. "My Eskimos down at Sitkee are modern as flying saucers. Some even been to college, and many don't mind talking real open about them old superstitions."

Glancing at his watch, he rose so quickly his chair fell over backward. "Time I was riding!"

They were walking him to his plane when he stopped to point at distant cliffs rising from the sea at the very tip of the big arm of land that went from the other side of the river. "Out there's what the Eskimos call The-Place-Where-the-Village-Died. They ever say anything to you about it?"

"Yes, when we first came. They said it was an ancient rule that no one should ever go out there. To break the rule would bring very bad luck."

Texas Andy nodded. "Same as they told me. When I get to thinking about that place it always puts me in mind of that feller Peters who owned the trading post here many years ago."

"Peters? Is he the one that disappeared so mysteriously?"

"That's him. Maybe he got lost in one of them

58

thick tundra fogs, or fell through the ice, or met up with a polar bear. Reckon nobody knows. The Eskimos that set out to find him soon came back."

"Couldn't they find his trail?" asked Mark.

"Oh, they found his trail, all right. But they was scared to follow. It led right out there to The-Place-Where-the-Village-Died."

6- beyond the river

THE BUSH pilot's red plane was a tiny speck in the southern sky when it turned and came back to fly low over the beach. Texas Andy waved, then dropped something white and fluttery that fell in the sand.

"It's a note!" yelled Milly.

Mark outraced her and picked up the folded paper tied to a rock. He cut the string with his hunting knife and read the message.

I just seen five boats going up the river. All loaded down. Must be going home. Now you can rest easy. Tex

Mark ran to meet his parents and read the message aloud. His father and mother looked at each other. His father grabbed the note and read it again.

"It's true, Helen," he said. "Anga was right. He was sure they would be leaving before the river froze."

Mark was surprised to see the look on his mother's face. Her eyes filled with tears. Her lips trembled. She turned quickly and hurried back toward the house.

"Mama!" screamed Milly, darting after her. But her father caught her as she tried to pass and lifted her in his strong arms.

"There now, she'll be all right in a few minutes," he said soothingly. "You see, darling, mothers are funny people. They never want us to know how worried they really are until everything is all right again."

61

He set her down gently. "Now you kids run along. Go check the gill nets. See if we've caught any salmon."

Mark gave his father a knowing look and, taking Milly's hand, led her away.

"Do you think Daddy was worried, too?" she asked in a small voice.

"Not him. He's a man! He's not afraid of anything." It was a good feeling to have in this lonely place where the sky and sea and tundra were so big and so endless that they made you feel like a tiny speck.

They went down to the sunny beach. It was usually the friendliest place in the village, but now it seemed empty and strange without the tumbling and laughter of Eskimo children, and the patient women mending their nets.

Dark-headed Sabine gulls were skimming low over the whitecaps. A fresh salt breeze had sprung up. It caught at the fat cushions of stranded sea foam and, breaking them up, spilled hundreds of fluffy foam balls across the sand. Mark kicked at them as they went scooting by.

It was no fun. Nothing was fun any more now that Oka was gone. He missed all the Eskimos, even the two old men who used to come into the trading post and sit for hours without saying a word.

During the next few lonely days Mark became more and more anxious about the fox cub, for the cries of Kali had not been heard for almost a week.

"Don't worry about it," his father had told him. "It probably means that Kali is beginning to enjoy his new life. He no longer needs you."

But Mark could not put the fox out of his mind. Kali could have been surprised by a snowy owl or an arctic wolf. Even his sealskin collar could become a choking snare and bring sudden death if it caught on a willow branch.

One day Mark was out gathering driftwood when he heard the yipping of a young fox. The yips came floating from a great distance. He held his breath until the faint yipping came again.

Was it Kali? There were many young foxes about, and they all did their share of yipping. Once again he heard the yips. There was something about them that made his heart beat faster. It could be Kali, but he had to be sure.

In a matter of minutes he had crossed the river in Anga's kayak. "This time I have to find him," he told himself as he scrambled up the far bank. "His collar is soon going to be too small. I have to take it off now because this may be the last chance I'll ever have."

Nothing stirred on the tundra beyond except the fowls in their marshes. There was no sign of Kali anywhere. He heard nothing but the distant wash of the sea and the honking of noisy flocks winging above in black-speck formations.

It seemed to him that the yipping had come from down by the sea beyond the cape, the great arm of land that curved out to sea from the mouth of the river. Mark hesitated. He did not want to get too far from the village. Yet he had to find Kali.

As he went on he wondered why it was that the Eskimos stayed away from this side of the river. What was it they feared? He couldn't believe there was any danger. He and his father had often taken walks over here. But they had never ventured out on the cape, for out near its tip, among the rocks and cliffs, was The-Place-Where-the-Village-Died.

Passing quickly beyond the cape Mark followed the curve of beach, looking for fox tracks in the wind-ribbed sand.

He gave a sharp whistle. Almost at once he saw

64

a flash of wings up ahead as several arctic terns rose in the air and came flying toward him, as if in answer to his call. Mark could hardly believe it. They came so close he could easily make out their dark caps and pointed red beaks. But suddenly they discovered him and veered sharply out over the sea.

He watched them, wondering why they had acted so strangely. If his whistle had frightened them they would have flown away from the sound, not toward him. Had they been frightened by something else, something farther up the beach?

He looked far up the beach, straining his eyes, wishing he had thought to bring his binoculars. Suddenly his eyes caught a movement. He lost it, then saw it again. It was coming closer and looked like a wisp of gray smoke skimming over the sand as if driven before the wind.

It was a fox cub, and it was streaking toward him along the beach.

"Kali!"

His voice choked. He fell to his knees and held out his arms.

But Kali did not leap into them. He sped past, turned, raced around and around. He leaped, he

65

danced, he pawed the air—yipping wildly all the while. His yips were the squeakiest, most breathless yips Mark had ever heard.

Mark held out his hand. "Come on, boy. Come, Kali."

The fox darted in, struck at the hand with a forepaw and flashed away, quick as a whisker's twitch.

"So that's it! You want to play." Mark got set with both hands. "All right. Come on now and I'll bat you down."

Then they went at it, playing the boxing game Kali loved.

He had grown. His legs were longer, more delicate-looking, and had the bounce of steel springs. They moved faster than the eye could follow as Kali flashed in and out, striking, leaping back, dodging Mark's clumsy blows.

Their play battle was loud with yips and laughter. Another fox cub appeared from behind a grassy mound. It joined in the yipping and began running about them in large circles. Before long still another young fox came to join the first.

The chorus of wild yippings attracted a snowy owl, several large burgomaster gulls, and a couple of hawklike jaegers. The birds made low passes overhead. The gulls and owl soon settled on rocks

66

some distance away. They had often dined on scraps of fur and feather after a fox had eaten its fill. They were content to await the outcome of this battle, too, in the hope that there might be a kill and a free meal.

Mark soon tired. He dropped flat on his back in the sand to catch his breath. But his eyes never left Kali, who circled once and came up cautiously to sniff at his boots and clothing.

Kali was no longer a house pet, used to being handled by people. He belonged to the open tundra now, and his quick alert movements were those of a wild animal.

"Come, Kali," Mark said softly, patting the sand by his head. "Come here and curl up like you used to do in my bunk."

Kali whined. He backed away a few steps and sat on his haunches, his ears pointed skyward, head cocked, and his red tongue lolling from the corner of his mouth. He wanted to come, but his wild nature had sharpened and made him wary. Mark closed his eyes and pretended to sleep.

Several minutes passed. Presently he was rewarded by the tickle of whiskers on his face and chin. The touch of a warm wet tongue on his neck brought a smile to his lips.

67

He opened his eyes. Would Kali jump away if he tried to pet him? Mark was almost afraid to try. With his heart pounding, he raised his hand and passed it ever so lightly along the gray-blue back of his pet.

The little fox did not seem to mind. Instead of being frightened it edged closer, as if the touch had stirred memories half forgotten and filled it with a trembling need to be petted.

Mark wanted to cry and laugh in the same breath. Kali was his again. Kali loved him and needed him still.

"Down, Kali." He pressed gently on the cub's back.

It snuggled down against his neck, and with a deep snuffling breath rested its head on his chest.

Filled with warm tenderness, Mark did not move for a long time. The owl and gulls still sat on the rocks. The two fox cubs had stopped their yipping. They were sitting quietly on their haunches only ten feet away, watching him curiously.

Mark smiled. It was as if the birds and animals of the tundra were all his friends and were keeping him company. The fox cubs had probably never seen a human being before, and didn't know enough to be afraid. They were puzzled about him, and Kali's confidence in him gave them courage.

As Mark was watching the young foxes they suddenly both jerked their heads about and stared intently at some rocks on the shore of the cape. Kali, too, jerked up his head to stare.

What had they heard? Mark sat up. Though he searched the rocks for several long moments he could see nothing unusual.

"You kids are just jumpy," he told the foxes. "There's nothing over on the cape now. The people with the strange boats have gone back up the river."

He took off Kali's sealskin collar and rubbed the neck and up behind the ears. Kali thanked him by nuzzling and licking his hands.

"Say, your ribs are sticking out," he said in alarm. "I'm going back to get you some salmon."

On the way to the river he tried to make the cub heel. But Kali had forgotten the command. He kept wandering off to one side or the other, sometimes scampering off to frolic with the other foxes, sometimes pausing to feed on moss berries.

"No wonder you're thin!" exclaimed Mark.

"You've been living on berries when you should have been learning to hunt. Now I'll have to fatten you up or you'll never live through the winter."

He brought back the largest salmon he could find on the drying racks, cut it into three large pieces and tossed one to each of the three fox cubs.

Almost at once the big gulls came out of nowhere.

"Keee-eeer! Keee-eeer!" they screamed. They dived so low that the fox cubs snarled and flattened their ears and tried to drag their fish into the thickets of willow brush.

At the dinner table that evening Mark told how he had to fight the gulls so the foxes could eat in peace. "I have to feed Kali fish every day now to fatten him up for winter."

His father reached for another helping of baked salmon. "The ice cellars are almost empty," he said. "If you're planning to feed the foxes you'll simply have to catch your own fish."

"I will. I'll set out a gill net," Mark promised. "Dad, can't I bring Kali back to the village? He wouldn't have to be chained now."

"No. When the Eskimos come back they'll be setting out traps for foxes on this side of the river. Kali would get caught. Over there on the other side he'll be safe enough until it's time for him to go out on the ice and hunt up a polar bear."

The words struck Mark like a club. He had completely forgotten that Kali would be leaving him again to spend the winter out on the frozen sea.

Milly shrieked with laughter. "Daddy, what you said! Who ever heard of a little old fox going out to hunt polar bears!"

Her mother laughed. "It isn't quite what you think, dear. The fox doesn't go out to eat polar bears."

"No, it's like this, Milly," explained her father. "In winter when the birds are gone, and most of the rabbits, there isn't much left for a fox to eat. So it goes out on the ice, finds a polar bear, and follows it around all winter to eat the seal meat the bear leaves behind."

Milly blinked. "You mean the fox steals the bear's dinner?"

"No. A seal is pretty big, more than a bear cares to eat. The bear eats off the thick layer of fat and leaves the rest. As soon as it goes away the fox has a feast."

"Won't the bear kill the fox?" she asked.

"The fox is much too fast for a polar bear," answered her father.

Mark said, "Dad, if I was to feed Kali every day he wouldn't leave me and follow some old bear, would he?"

"Probably not. But what would you feed him all through the winter?"

"Fish. When it freezes I'll put a net under the ice, like the Eskimos do," said Mark. "And I'll start storing fish in an ice cellar right now."

His father smiled. "If Kali means that much to you then go right ahead."

7- when the village died

TEXAS ANDY dropped down out of the sky several days later. He had flown a sick Eskimo woman to the hospital at Barrow, he said, and was now on his way home.

"You wouldn't come seventy miles out of your way just to pay us a friendly call," said Mark, glancing up at his tall friend as they walked toward the trading post. "You got some special reason for coming."

Texas Andy laughed. "It was kind of accidental-like. I was having such a good time herding them clouds around up there I drifted off course. When I looked down and saw your village I figured to set down awhile and dust my feathers."

The bush pilot's joshing made Mark more positive than ever there was a special reason for the visit. But not until they had finished dinner and the men had lighted cigars did Texas Andy finally get to the point of his visit.

"I been asking around about the people who came down the river in them boats," he said. "Old Judah, who used to live here years ago, says they come from somewhere in the Brooks Mountains. In bad years, when caribou herds don't go through the mountain passes, these people have nothing much to hunt so they come down the river to fish for a while."

Mark's father slapped the table. "I knew it was something like that. Those Eskimos don't bring

74

bad luck. They simply come when caribou hunting is poor."

Mark's mother said, "That doesn't explain why our Eskimos are afraid of them. What are those mountain Eskimos like, Tex?"

The pilot blew a puff of cigar smoke toward the ceiling. "That's mighty big country up there north of the Yukon. There's many Eskimo tribes living up there in them mountain passes. I hear some of them still hunt with bows and arrows and follow the orders of witch doctors. Here's the story old Judah told me about the tribe that come down here in them boats."

The story began a hundred years or so ago and told of savage battles between two Eskimo tribes. One of these tribes, the Seal People, had lived right here where the village now stood; and the enemy tribe lived in the village at the end of the cape only six miles away. Like so many tribal wars of that ancient time this one went on and on endlessly. And all through those bitter years the river Sitkin had stood as a line between their tribal hunting grounds.

A few killings now and then were to be expected. But there were seasons for killing the enemy, and

75

seasons for hunting. These seasons never came at the same time, for it was the first law of the tundra that men had to hunt while hunting was good. The caribou and seal and walrus and whale each came in its season, and none of them could be expected to wait while men battled among themselves.

The hunting season was always a time of peace among men. It was a time when villages could be left unguarded while the men went forth to hunt for their food.

It was during one of these times of peace that terror gripped the Seal People. Two of their hunters were struck down by enemy arrows one day while they were out on the ice at the seal holes. When this news reached the village the stunned people quickly gathered in the large community house of sod and whalebone. Their way of life was being threatened. If men had to guard themselves and their village during the hunting season, then death by starvation was all that was left for them.

The Seal People struck back that very night. They knew exactly where the enemy hunters would be, for in those days only the women and children lived in the small sod houses. All the men lived in the community house in the center of the village.

The Seal People closed swiftly on the community house, blocked the entrance, then shot their arrows down through the smoke hole in the roof.

In the confusion of battle most of the enemy women and children escaped by dog sleds. But all the enemy hunters were killed that night and their village was left in ruins.

So peace came, and the years flew by like flakes of snow in the white wind. Strange ships came with men who had white skin. They brought steel knives and guns and iron kettles, and these they offered to trade for skins of the arctic fox.

In time the village of the Seal People became known as Cape North. Every year a white missionary came and taught them songs and stories of the Christian God. It was wrong for the Seal People to follow the spirit of the seals, he explained; and it was wrong for them to listen to the words of witch doctors.

Now the witch doctor of that time was called Tornick. He was young, and as yet the people had no great fear of his magic powers. But Tornick feared the missionary's words would destroy him. He placed a curse on the missionary to keep him away from the village. When the curse failed it was clear to all that the Christian God was stronger than the spirit of the seals. The missionary turned the people against Tornick and had him banished forever from the village.

Tornick left, screaming that he would have his revenge. Shortly after that the mysterious murders began. Two or three hunters were killed every year, and these killings always took place beyond the river on land which had once belonged to the enemy tribe.

In time it was learned that Tornick had joined the enemy tribe in the mountains and boasted that these killings were only the beginning of his terrible revenge. The day would come, he promised, when he would lead his people out of the mountains to destroy the village of Cape North in a single night.

Texas Andy had finished the strange tale he had heard from old Judah. He lighted his cigar again. "All that goes back many years. There's been no killing around here for a long, long time."

Mark's father leaned forward. "Why didn't Tornick carry out his threat to destroy the village?"

"Bows and arrows wouldn't have much chance against village guns. Tornick had to take his tribe deep in the mountains and keep them away from other tribes and white people. That was the only way he could keep them in his power. But he must be dead by now."

"What shocks me," said Mark's mother, "is that our own Eskimos thought so little of our safety that they left us behind. We might all have been killed."

"You're plumb wrong, Helen," replied Texas Andy. "If there was any danger of a raid it would have come when all the Eskimos were right here in the village. They knew you'd be a heap safer with them gone, and I'm certain sure that's one reason they cleared out so fast."

Mr. McRoy pushed back his chair. "I simply can't believe there's any real danger now. After all, these are modern times. Eskimo wars are a thing of the past."

"That's what I figure," agreed Texas Andy. "Them people who came in the boats didn't mean no harm. All this trouble would have been over forty years ago if it hadn't been for that crazy witch doctor. All he lived for was to get revenge."

8- a black-
feathered arrow

FOR MARK the village was a lonely place without
Oka and the other Eskimo boys. It surprised him
that he could miss them so much. His happiest

80

hours each day were those he spent with Kali on the tundra beyond the river. The two friendly fox cubs, which he named Tip and Tap, usually tagged along. They seemed to enjoy his company and loved the bits of fish he always brought for them.

Sometimes they were joined by two other cubs and a vixen, who was probably the mother of all four cubs. The vixen was larger and more timid than the young, and her blue-gray coat had faded to tawny yellow on her underside.

One afternoon when the vixen was along, she stopped suddenly. Her soft throat noises instantly drew the attention of the cubs. She started away on a swift glide, and her cubs and Kali followed, silent and eager, each trying to imitate the swift, smooth run of the mother fox. The vixen had taken complete command. Once again she was giving her cubs a lesson in hunting.

Through brush and patches of heather and reindeer moss the vixen darted in a series of swift runs, stopping short now and then to peer ahead and to test the breeze with her sensitive nose. One of the cubs edged up to run at its mother's side. She wheeled and drove it back with a snarl and a slash of punishing teeth.

Her worried backward glances warned Mark to

keep back. He did. He followed a hundred yards behind, moving through black clouds of mosquitoes stirred up by the passing foxes.

The vixen reached the edge of the beach and whisked down behind a drift of sand, then made for a group of rocks near the sea. She bellied up behind a rock at the water's edge. The little foxes followed and took up positions behind other rocks. Mark hid behind a grassy mound and watched them through his binoculars. His heart was thumping. He had no idea what the vixen was after, but he noticed she was looking out over the sea.

He studied the sea. Beyond the breakers arctic trout were leaping and making silvery splashes in the lazy green swells. But they were far out of reach for the foxes. Mark was more puzzled than ever.

He noticed the long-tailed robber gulls flying back and forth over the water. They, too, were taking an interest in the leaping trout, for they were expert fishers. When they were not flying over the tundra, robbing nests of eggs and young, they were almost sure to be skimming over the heaving sea, looking for fish near the surface.

One of the birds wheeled in a tight circle. It paused in mid-air, spreading its tail so wide it made a fork. Suddenly, folding its wings, it went down in a clean dive. There was an explosion of white spray, and the bird appeared with a trout in its strong, hooked beak.

But the fish was too large to be lifted out of the sea. The robber gull made for shore, half swimming, half flying, as it trailed the thrashing fish through the water.

It reached the breakers and was lost from sight in the flying spray. But somehow it came through and finally dragged the flopping trout well up on the sand.

At that moment the vixen began her charge. She covered the distance like the flick of a shadow. With a rush of wings the gull took to the air, screeching in panic. The fox pounced on the fish, caught it up in her narrow jaws and came trotting up the beach to bury it in the sand.

Again and again the big robber gulls brought their fish ashore, only to lose them to the waiting foxes. When the cubs tired of their fishing lesson the vixen began dragging rocks to cover the spot where the fish were buried.

Mark went down to the beach to watch her work, which did not please her at all. He noticed that Kali had dug a shallow hole in the sand and was chewing on something white. A bone? No, it looked more like a piece of carved ivory. He took it from Kali.

To his surprise he found it to be a beautifully carved sitting fox. Every detail was perfect. Glancing into the hole Kali had dug he saw torn bits of leather that had probably once been an Eskimo charm bag.

"I'm going to make a charm bag and wear this because you gave it to me," he told Kali. "Maybe it will bring me luck."

He gathered driftwood and, with Kali at his heels, set off on a gallop across the tundra. Everywhere about him fluffy balls of the cotton grass stood up on slender stems like thousands of white flowers. By closing his eyes a little, he could make the cotton balls look like stars, and imagine himself flying through space on the Milky Way.

He made his fire in a patch of heather because heather was good to burn. Tip and Tap came trotting up. He gave them and Kali a part of his fried duck-egg sandwich.

"Sit by the fire, Kali," he said, forcing the cub to sit beside him. "I made it so you'd get used to campfires. We're going to have lots of them this winter. You're not going to spend your winter tagging after some old bear out there on the ice."

Kali nuzzled his hand, and the soft wet look in his eyes gave Mark the feeling of being understood.

For some reason Tip and Tap seemed unusually restless. They kept jumping up to look this way and that.

The wind from the sea freshened. It brought the chill of the ice fields and weaving banners of fog.

"I'll bet you kids are uneasy because of the fog," he told the cubs. The sound of his voice usually calmed them. But it did not do so now.

Kali remained perfectly calm. He was too busy begging for bits of cookie to be disturbed about anything. Mark took the cub in his lap. "I guess you know I'll protect you if there's any danger, don't you."

But Tip and Tap continued their restless shifting. Mark began to feel uneasy himself. There was only one thing that might disturb the other cubs more than it would Kali—and that thing was man.

There was no hint of life on the tundra beyond the fire. In all that sweep of empty land nothing moved except the wisps of fog that came floating in from the sea like so many shapeless ghosts. Mark studied the low brush, the screens of marsh grass and the moss-covered boulders. They were places where a man could hide.

The prickly feeling at the back of his neck told him someone was out there. Someone was watching him. Several times lately he had felt he was being watched.

Kali suddenly sprang from his lap. He stood facing the wind, reading it with his sharp nose. The long hair on his back and neck stood straight up like a brush. A growl rumbled in his throat.

"What is it, boy?" Mark whispered. "You smell something?"

In the raw mist that was closing down it was impossible to see clearly. The distant rocks and brush patches were shadowy forms in a swirl of gray. But as Mark watched, one of the forms began to move and to take shape.

It was coming closer. He suddenly recognized what it was, and his heart leaped like a snowshoe rabbit.

The form that came loping out of the mist, its head bobbing low each time its forefeet struck the ground, was a great white wolf of the Arctic.

It paused some distance away and stood looking at them.

Once again a low growl came from Kali. Tap's ears were flat back. She bared her teeth and snarled. Tip whined. He was trembling, and he moved back and forth as though he wanted to run away, or move closer to the fire, and was much too frightened to do either one.

Mark sat as still as a tundra stone. From the corner of his eye he watched as the shadowy form moved. It faded. It circled in the mist to pick up their scent on the down-wind side.

When it caught the man smell it would probably

drift away, Mark told himself. Arctic wolves did not attack people. At least so the Eskimos said. But there was always a chance that this wolf was mad, or did not know about men and their guns.

For the first time in his life Mark missed his gun. It was a fine 30.30, which his father had given him for Christmas; and it still had its new oily smell. He had never used it for anything except target practice down at the beach.

But having a rifle at home did not help him now. He took out his knife to have it ready. Only one piece of driftwood remained by the fire. It was too small to be used as a club.

Minutes passed. The wolf did not go away. It moved quietly about them, first one way, then the other. It came closer and closer, until Mark could see the evil slant of its yellow eyes.

The eyes never gave him more than a wary glance. The wolf was watching the fox cubs. It had probably dined on many a baby fox during the summer.

Arctic foxes were faster than wolves, Mark knew. But he wondered if his half-grown cubs were speedy enough to save themselves.

Kali was taking no chances. He stood with his back pressed against Mark. Tap stood only inches away. Even little Tip had come within three feet, and stood closer to the fire than ever before.

They all kept their eyes fixed on the great white beast. It sat down on its haunches less than twenty feet away. Mark knew it might keep them pinned down by the fire for many hours—maybe all through the night.

Mark began gathering heather to throw on the fire. So long as the flames were bright the wolf would not dare come much closer. But to keep the fire burning would take lots of fuel. On hands and knees he worked around the fire, ripping up all the heather within reach. It made only a small heap, not enough to keep the fire going for more than half an hour.

Once again the wolf faded into the mist. It swung wide and came slinking up behind him.

"It's getting bolder because it thinks I can't do anything," Mark thought. "If I could give it a good scare it might go away."

The piece of driftwood gave him an idea. He held one end of it in the fire until it became a flaming torch. Then, springing to his feet, he rushed at the crouching beast, yelling at the top of his voice. He tried to ram the torch into the great jaws. But the wolf leaped aside.

89

Just as Mark charged it again one of the foxes broke from the fire and went dashing off across the tundra. The big wolf was after it in an instant.

Mark ran back to the fire. Tip was missing. Kali and Tap stood frozen, watching the chase.

The wolf covered the ground in mighty leaps. But Tip had a good start and seemed to be holding his lead. They were almost out of sight in the mist when Tip suddenly turned to run in a circle. He had changed his mind and was trying to get back to the fire.

Mark held his breath. He could see that Tip was not going to make it. The wolf was cutting him off.

The end came quickly. In one of its great leaps the white wolf suddenly took a flip. It spun head over heels in mid-air and landed heavily on its back. It did not get up again.

Stunned, Mark watched the still form for several minutes. Why was the wolf lying so still? What had happened to it?

Slowly, with the driftwood stick in one hand and his hunting knife held ready in the other, he approached the place where the great beast lay. It did not seem to be breathing. He poked at it with his stick. It did not move.

Kali and Tap came up to sniff and yip angrily. They had suddenly become very bold.

So far as Mark could see there was no wound. Yet the wolf seemed to be dead. It had died in mid-air, as though struck down by some invisible force.

"There must be a wound on the other side," Mark said aloud.

He took hold of a leg and rolled the limp animal over.

For a frozen moment he stared in amazement. He backed away, one slow step, then another. Suddenly he spun around to run for home as fast as he could. Terror raced with him, for, buried deep in the hairy chest, he had seen the giver of death—a black-feathered arrow.

In the kitchen lamplight Mark saw fear stiffen his mother's face as he told her what had happened.

"That settles it," she said. "You are not going over there again, Mark!"

He sank in a chair. "Kali is over there. How can I see him if—" He broke off as he thought of the black-feathered arrow.

"It's best not to take chances," his father said. "Our Eskimos weren't nearly as superstitious as we thought. They knew some of those people might be living over there at almost any time of the year, so they simply stay on this side to avoid trouble."

"I don't like it," said Mrs. McRoy, moving a steaming pot to the back of the stove. "The way that witch doctor took those people back in the mountains and kept them living like savages all these years. . . . Why, there's no telling what they might do!"

"They haven't caused trouble for many years," said Mark's father. "Texas Andy says Tornick must be dead."

"But he doesn't know! I have a feeling Tornick is still alive. He'd be old now. If he still plans to wipe out this village some night he'll have to do it soon. We—we can't go on living in this place. Can't you see?"

"This trading post is all we have in the world, Helen. It's our living. Our life. I'd be ruined if we were to leave."

"But the children!" said Mark's mother. "Why can't we send them to Wisconsin?"

His father took a turn about the room. "It may be the thing to do. I don't know. I'd have to borrow money from Tex to do it."

Mark closed his eyes. He wanted to plug his

ears, too. The black-feathered arrow had done more than kill a wolf. It had put Kali out of reach. And now he and Milly might have to leave their parents and go back to Wisconsin. He'd not see Oka or any of his other Eskimo friends again. There was not much left for him to care about.

9- Mark's sudden plane ride

SEPTEMBER was a month of many changes. On the beach an uneasy peace had fallen between the foxes and the gulls. Thousands of small shrimps were washing up on the sand every day, and the birds and foxes were feasting side by side like polite strangers.

September brought trouble for the tundra chickens. They had already turned white, and because they were easy to see against the brown of the tundra they could no longer hide themselves from the hungry owls. It was a month when winds swept in from the sea to pluck at the fluffy tops of the cotton grass.

The moss berries had ripened. Even Mark's mother could enjoy berry picking now, for killing frosts had cleared the air of swarming mosquitoes. Milly's wounded snow bunting had recovered the use of its wing and left her to join the other buntings, who were gathering in flocks for their southward flight.

By the end of September several of the older Eskimos had already returned to the village. Two small Eskimo girls came with them. The girls joined Mark and Milly each morning for two hours of school at the kitchen table.

"Three or four more pupils should be back in another week or so," Mrs. McRoy told the children. "Then we'll move to the schoolhouse and have regular school hours."

Even the hope of seeing her friend Tani soon again did not cheer Milly. "In another week," she told Mark, "we might be on our way back to Wisconsin."

Mark did not want to think about going back to his grandfather's farm. But he saw how worried his mother was and knew she had not changed her mind.

He tried to earn the right to stay by doing the work of a man. He helped his father clean stove-pipes, and whitewashed the walls of the bunkroom and kitchen. He and his father spent a day repairing the floor of the trading post, and all the while he tried to make good man-to-man talk.

"Dad," he said, "you wouldn't sell the trading post, would you?"

"Nobody wants to buy a business that's losing money. No, in bad times like this I have to stick it out or I'll lose everything."

Mark steadied the board his father was sawing. The smell of fresh pine lumber mingled with the fragrance of coffee and spices in the grocery part of the trading post. Mark said, "Then you have to stay here. I'll be old enough to help you a lot this winter."

"I hope it works out that way," said his father thoughtfully.

Mark knew his father was still thinking about sending him back to Wisconsin. He reached for the charm bag at his throat and rubbed the carved ivory fox with his fingers, just for luck. To leave the secret tundra world he and Kali had shared, to leave Oka and his parents and friends—why, it would be like dying! He couldn't leave. He wouldn't!

"I know what, Dad. Let's get a radio sending set. Then Mom won't have to worry. We could send for help right away if the mountain Eskimos came back."

"I'd have had one long ago if they weren't so expensive. We'll just have to wait awhile for that."

"But think how much it will cost sending us kids back to Wisconsin. And sending us back won't help. The danger will still be here. Mother will still be worried. If there's going to be a battle we need everyone who can shoot a rifle right here in the village. You said yourself I was a good shot. I even beat you the last time we had target practice."

His father took a deep breath. "Yes. I know. The Eskimos and all of us are in this together. But the only real danger I see has to do with your mother's health. You know how she worries."

"Maybe she won't worry so much when the Eskimos get back," said Mark. He knew that some of the Eskimo families could be expected back soon so that their children wouldn't miss too much school. Mark tapped a board into place and nailed it down.

He remembered his mother had said she had a strong feeling Tornick, the witch doctor, was still alive. He could feel things, too, and the Eskimos seemed to feel a lot of things they couldn't see. But did feelings tell the truth?

"Dad, the Eskimos are always talking about the spirit of wild foxes, the spirit of caribou, things like that. Are those just Eskimo superstitions? Couldn't there be angels watching over animals?"

His father measured off another length of board. "Angels watching over animals?"

"Well, sometimes when Kali and I were alone on the tundra we felt something—something friendly and close to us." He ran his hand over the new pine flooring. "It sounds crazy, I guess."

"No," his father said softly. "Out there on the tundra a man can feel many things. Sometimes his feelings lie to him, sometimes they don't."

"The good feelings must be true. I had a good feeling today because Kali is hunting near the river. He goes away for three or four days at a time. But he always comes back to hunt near the river."

"Just how do you know that?"

"Whenever he's near I keep waking up nights. I can hear his yapping over there."

"That's nonsense, Mark. Foxes are yapping over there every night."

"Kali yaps longer. It's as if he was calling me. This morning I saw him with the binoculars. I knew it was him because he always keeps looking over this way."

Mark did not add that he often threw fish on the far bank from Anga's kayak on days when Kali was near. Not that his father would have minded, for they were his own fish. One of his first tasks each morning was to tend his gill net in the river. That would be harder to do now with the river freezing over. He continued storing fish in an ice cellar just as though he were still planning to feed Kali all through the winter. It didn't hurt to hope, and hoping made the long, lonely days easier to bear.

In October there was less time for loneliness. The Eskimos began coming back in family groups, one after another. Oka's family was one of the last to return and, much to Mark's disappointment, Oka and his uncle had to leave again almost at once to haul home their harvest of fish from the fishing camp.

With arctic winter almost upon them, all the Eskimos were in a hurry to get things done. Freshwater ice had to be cut from a tundra lake before the ice became too thick. Mark and his father helped. The ice blocks were hauled home on dog sleds and stored by the trading post and the Eskimo houses, so that each family would have fresh water enough to last them through the winter.

Oka returned with his last load of fish just in time to join Mark and the Eskimos who were going to the coal-mining place twenty miles up the river. The mine was an open pit in the bank of the river. While the men dug with picks, the boys broke up the large lumps with hammers and shoveled the coal into sacks, which were then hauled down the river on dog sleds.

Mark didn't mind the hard work. He was happy to be with Oka again. They had so much to tell each other, and they had so many plans to make for their winter camp.

It was a bitter cold day late in November. A thin slice of moon, and frosty stars, shone down on the people gathered about Texas Andy's plane on the river ice.

Mark edged a little closer when he saw his father talking to the bush pilot.

"Well, if you're coming back next week—" his father was saying.

"I have to be back next week, and a couple more times before Christmas. Everybody's giving me Christmas orders to fill." Texas Andy lowered his voice. "Don't worry none about them kids of yours. By next week your wife might change her mind. If she don't, I'll take the kids with me then and see that they get down to Wisconsin."

"Thanks, Tex," his father said, shaking the pilot's hand. "I'm still hoping they won't have to go. We'd miss them a lot. Mark, here, is just getting old enough to be a real help to me. He's been working like a man."

The warmth of his father's praise made Mark wish he had worked even harder.

Texas Andy measured him with squinty eyes. "Beats all how kids grow. First thing you know he'll be off with the hunters to earn his keep."

"Well," Mr. McRoy said slowly, "I'll say this for him: He's a crack shot."

But he did not add that Mark rarely shot at anything except tin cans and driftwood targets. Mark blushed. He did not dare glance at the Eskimos because he felt sure they were all watching him and thinking things they were too polite to say.

Oka tried to defend him. "Mark and me got a hunting camp six miles up the river. We go there

101

every Friday after school and stay one night and one day."

At that moment old Anga came up with a last-minute Christmas order. Mark breathed easier. When no one was looking he ducked under the tail of the plane, slipped into the cabin on the other side and crawled back into the gloom, among the mail sacks and packing cases.

A moment later Texas Andy took his seat and slammed the door. The engine roared. The little ship trembled. With a jolt it leaped ahead, gathering speed on the broad runway of river ice.

Mark crawled forward and climbed into the seat beside the pilot. "Got to talk to you," he shouted, above the roar of the engine.

"Knew you was there all the time," said the pilot cheerfully. "I'll run you up the river a piece. Then we can set down a spell."

The plane rose in the air. For a minute it skimmed low over the snow-covered tundra, avoiding two large bends in the river, and then settled once again on the river ice.

"It's about my mother," Mark began. "She's a lot more worried than Dad thinks. Three days ago I heard one of the women tell her that lots of enemy Eskimos are keeping watch on the other side of the river, more than ever before. Since then she can't keep her mind on the work at school. She hardly eats at all, except when Dad is watching her. It won't help if Milly and I go to Wisconsin. Then she'd only worry herself sick about Dad and business and the Eskimo kids."

Texas Andy nodded thoughtfully. "She'd be better off down in Wisconsin with you kids, I reckon."

"She wouldn't think of leaving Dad. What worries her most up here is that there's no way we could call for help if anything happened. That's why I thought of you. Remember that little emergency sending set you carried that time your plane radio was out of order?"

"I still got it at home," said Texas Andy. "But you can't send messages with it. When you turn the crank it just sends out a buzzing signal over and over. Other planes could locate me by that buzzing in case I crashed somewhere."

"I know," said Mark. "That's all we need. We wouldn't have to send any messages. We wouldn't turn the crank unless we needed help bad. Couldn't you let us borrow it for a while?"

Texas Andy's face lighted up. "Sure thing. I'd be proud to let you use it. And any time I hear your buzzing signal on my plane radio I'll come high-tailing it up here fast as I can."

"I knew you'd help. I bet Mom won't worry half so much when we get that sending set. The main thing she wants is for us to be able to call for help if we need it." Mark sat back and took the first deep breath he'd been able to take in several days. "Everything would be swell now if it wasn't for Kali."

"Kali? You mean that little pet fox of yourn?"

"Yes. I can't go over and be with him on the other side of the river, you know, and I don't want him to come near the village where the Eskimos have set out all those fox traps. He doesn't yap for me near as often now."

"You talk to Anga about it?"

"I wouldn't dare talk to any of the Eskimos about it. I—I'd feel ashamed. They don't understand about me and Kali. They think pets are only for little kids."

"I reckon they do." As if to stir up some luck Texas Andy ran his hand along the row of rabbits' feet dangling like a fringe above his windshield. "It's hard living that makes Eskimos that way. A thing has to have a good practical use or they figure it ain't worth nothing."

"I know." Mark stared up at the tundra sky. It

104

was as big as the feeling of hopelessness within him. But suddenly he brightened. "Maybe—maybe I could train Kali to do something useful!"

"That little feller's no bigger'n a snowshoe rabbit," Texas Andy reminded him. "Ain't nothing he could do that a dog couldn't do better."

It was true. Kali was much too small to pull a sled or to serve as a pack animal. "But what am I going to do? What can I do?"

"Let me figure on it for a few days. You do the same." Texas Andy looked at his watch. "It's time for me to be riding."

From the river ice Mark gave a final wave as his friend took off. He felt better, knowing he had found a way to lessen his mother's worries. And Texas Andy might be able to help solve his problem with Kali. But there wasn't much time left to find an answer, for in a week or two Kali and his fox friends would be heading out over the frozen sea to spend the winter with the polar bears.

Polar bears! Mark suddenly remembered his rifle. It was back in the village, over a mile away. Now that the sea was frozen and polar bears sometimes came ashore, Mark had strict orders to carry his rifle whenever he left the village.

He quickened his steps. Following the river he watched the rim of the tundra on both sides. Bears did not come ashore often.   But if one did, and it should happen to see him. . . . He shivered at the thought.

He had almost reached the first sweeping bend of the river when he suddenly caught his breath. Something white was moving up there along the snowy edge of the tundra.

Then he saw it clearly—an arctic fox.   In its new winter coat it looked frosty white in the moonlight. It ran above the bank of the river for several yards and then disappeared.

Forgetting his sudden fright, Mark raced up the bank after it.

10- howling wolf packs

A HUNDRED yards ahead he saw the fox trotting away. It made a wide turn to the left and continued turning until it was headed once again for the river.

Mark felt sure it was Kali. It had to be, or it wouldn't be coming toward him. He wanted to shout Kali's name. But something stopped him. Something wasn't quite right. The fox was still swinging to the left, still running in a great curve. It passed within a hundred feet of him as it swung away from the river.

It hadn't noticed him at all!

Once again the fox swung slowly back toward the river. Puzzled, Mark kept as still as he could, watching the animal's strange behavior. It was running around and around, each circle a little smaller than the last.

At the exact center of the circles lay several large rocks. The fox did not seem interested in them, but Mark knew foxes were much too smart to be running in dizzy circles just for exercise. This fox was doing some acting. It was pretending not to notice the rocks. Yet it was working slowly in toward those rocks as it ran in smaller and smaller circles.

Finally, as it came within four feet of an opening between the rocks, it turned sharply. Mark saw only a blur of white as it leaped among the rocks.

There was a squeal, an explosion of snow . . . then silence.

The long, lonely howl of an arctic wolf broke the winter stillness. It came from far up the river. Another wolf answered, and another, and still another. A whole chorus of wolf howls rent the air as Mark listened. He hadn't heard that many wolves in a long time. The wolf packs were running. Could it mean the caribou herds were coming back?

He knew the howling of the wolves was certain

to cause a great stir of excitement in the village. The Eskimos had very little caribou meat. Less than twenty of the big tundra deer had fallen to the guns of village hunters. At least a hundred more would be needed to keep the Eskimos supplied with fat and meat through the winter.

Once again the distant howling of wolves came floating across the barrens. But among the rocks where the white fox had made its kill there was no sound, no movement.

Mark approached the rocks quietly. He came within thirty feet before he saw the fox. It was feeding on a white snowshoe rabbit.

"Hello, there!" he called softly.

Up came the beautiful white head, showing dark round eyes and a black nose. The fox looked at him for a moment, then returned to its kill.

"I knew you weren't Kali," said Mark. "Kali always cocks his head when he looks at me like that. And you aren't a strange white fox either. A strange fox wouldn't trust me. He'd snarl and try to drag the rabbit away."

The fox went to work on a bone, crunching and cracking with its narrow jaws. But every now and then it rolled its eyes toward him to see that he came no closer.

Mark chuckled. It was fun being with one of his

tundra friends again. "You are Tap, or one of her sisters who used to hunt with us. You sure had that rabbit fooled. You passed so many times it must have thought it was hidden real good and wasn't in any danger."

He moved a few steps closer. The fox did not seem disturbed.

"Now I know you are Tap!"

The discovery gave him a light-headed feeling, for Kali and Tip and Tap usually hunted in the same area. Kali could not be many miles away, and would probably remain near the river for several days.

"Tap, you listen to me," he said, suddenly bursting with new plans. "This is my chance to get Kali back. Tomorrow I'm going to bring a whitefish and leave it here by the rocks. You'll find it when you come back to eat the rest of that rabbit. I'll bring fish every day. Let Kali and Tip have some, too. Keep them around till Friday afternoon. Will you do that?"

Tap licked her chops and yawned. She had eaten her fill. Springing lightly to the top of a boulder, she sat on her haunches, curled her silvery tail around her forepaws, and regarded him with sleepy eyes.

110

With a laugh and a wave Mark left her and went galloping for home across the snow. The plan was so simple, so perfect. He would take Kali to his hunting camp and make a home for him there. Then they could be together every week end.

In the slant of moonlight up ahead he saw track marks in the snow, Eskimo tracks. He suddenly remembered then that he was on the wrong side of the river, the forbidden side beyond the west bank of the Sitkin.

The tracks were fresh. Three Eskimos of the enemy tribe had passed that way only minutes ago. They had been running toward the place where the plane had landed on the river ice.

He knew they must have seen him leave the plane. Had they followed him? Were they watching him now? He thought again of the mysterious black-feathered arrow as he took a quick glance around and made a dash for the river. He ran most of the way home.

Behind him on the frozen barrens, wolves were still raising their voices in lonely, quivering howls. The village Eskimos had read the meaning of those howls and were shouting and laughing and hurrying this way and that in great excitement.

He saw dark clusters of children at the ice cellars. They were hauling up frozen fish, which would be packed on the dog sleds and would serve as trail food for the men and their dogs during the big caribou hunt.

Bright showers of sparks swirled up from the stovepipes above the sod Eskimo igloos. Eskimo women were stoking the fires in their oil-drum stoves. They were preparing hot meals for their husbands, who would soon be coming in from their seal holes on the ice.

Children were crawling in and out of the long snow entrance tunnels to their homes. They were all in a hurry. Some ran off to the trading post. Some went for driftwood. Others went for chunks

112

of lake ice, which would be melted down in fresh-water drums behind the stoves.

"Hey, Mark!" shouted one of the boys as he came from an entrance tunnel. "Get your gun! We all go hunt the caribou."

The boy went racing down to the beach to meet his father; for like all Eskimo boys he was thrilled at the thought of going hunting with the men.

Mark told himself he didn't care. He wasn't going caribou hunting. Yet it hurt to stay behind, to miss something all the others seemed to enjoy so much. They would be talking about the hunt for months, and he'd have to listen and not say a word. The worst of it was that he'd be the only big boy left in school—just he and the girls and little kids.

"They don't need me," he told himself. "Nothing is going to spoil my plan to get Kali back. I wouldn't be any good on a hunting trip anyway."

He decided not to tell his mother about the little wireless sending set. Only the set itself could ease her fears. When Texas Andy brought it next week they could surprise her with it.

For the next hour or so Mark was kept busy in the trading post. Almost everybody wanted such things as coffee, tea, sugar, dried fruits, tobacco, and ammunition—trail supplies for the hunters.

Oka came in when the rush was over. "You want to go caribou hunting, Mark?" he asked eagerly. "Joseph and Papanick say we can go with them."

"I'm not going," Mark said under his breath.

Oka's big smile disappeared. "This may be our only chance to hunt caribou. Now the big herds go south. We don't see them again till spring."

Mark still refused. But he tried to smooth things over a little by saying, "Maybe we could hunt caribou near our winter camp next Friday."

Oka looked at him in the strangest way, then swiftly left the store. Mark did not see him again because all the hunters left early the next morning.

It had become still and bitterly cold during the night. The temperature continued to drop for the next two days. Sharp reports, like the cracking of rifle fire, came from the barrens as frost bit deeper and deeper into the frozen earth. The sea ice boomed and split and rumbled. Sometimes it filled the air with mighty sounds like rushing trains and a dozen thunderstorms all going at once. At the trading post the wall timbers made splitting and snapping noises.

Going to school mornings, Mark and Milly covered their noses with their fur mittens. But even so the small hairs in their nostrils were soon frozen

114

stiff. Then every breath felt as if tickling straws were being shoved up their noses. They had to sneeze again and again. The sneezing fits brought tears, and the tears froze on their cheeks before they could reach the schoolhouse.

In school all the children kept on their caribou parkas and trousers, and huddled about the pot-bellied iron stove for warmth.

Mark's mother would say, "We'll start off with some warming music."

Tani played brisk marching records on the pho-nograph while the children sang and marched in an endless line about the stove, stamping their feet and clapping their hands until they tingled with warmth and good cheer.

It was usually an hour or so before the large room was warm enough to shed fur clothing. The whole north wall of the room was glazed over with ice that glistened in the light of the three Coleman lanterns.

There was no use trying to write. Frozen chalk wouldn't work on frozen blackboards. The ink in their fountain pens was frozen. Even the pencils slipped over paper without leaving a mark, for at the end of each lead point was a bead of ice.

Since Mark was the only big boy left in school—all the others having gone on the caribou hunt—it was his job to keep the coal buckets filled and to tend the fire. When he tried to study, his thoughts kept drifting back to his pet fox on the tundra.

He had followed his plan faithfully. Each day after school he covered his face with a layer of grease, just as Eskimos did in extremely cold weather, and took a frozen whitefish out to the rocks where Tap had made her kill.

There were many fox tracks at the feeding place, and the fish were eaten as fast as he brought them. Well-fed foxes were not likely to wander far from their feeding place. He felt certain they were sleeping in the clumps of sedge grass not far away, and would come at his call when he wanted them.

Most of the caribou hunters came back late on Thursday, after three disappointing days on the tundra. Many hunters had seen caribou, but the herds were traveling fast.

Oka told all about the hunt as he and Mark headed upriver for their hunting camp on Friday afternoon.

"Wolves make the caribou plenty scared," he complained. "We tried to get close to one herd. But in the cold weather like now our steps make the snow squeak loud, even when we wear the fur pads on our feet. The caribou hear the squeaking a mile away, and they turn their tails and run fast."

Mark dropped back to steady the supply sled as Oka pulled it over a small snowbank at the curve of the river. Moonlight flooded the glistening white world about them with milky brightness. Off to the right came a sharp report that sounded like gunfire. But Mark knew it was only the noise of frost cracking the frozen tundra.

"You fellows did shoot three caribou," Mark reminded him. "How did you do that?"

"It was only lucky accident. We saw caribou coming. We wait very still. Don't move, don't make sound. When they come close, we shoot. But then we came home because Papanick say hunting no good till weather change and snow don't squeak so much."

"The weather hasn't changed much yet," said Mark, secretly hoping it wouldn't. If the weather remained cold, Oka might not hold him to his promise to go caribou hunting, and then he would have more time to spend with Kali. As yet he had not dared say a word to Oka about Kali. Oka was not going to like having the fox in camp.

"We hunt all day tomorrow, Mark," Oka said. "You make the promise to hunt with me. Remember?"

Mark remembered all right. He did not know what to say.

"This time we have better luck," Oka said cheerfully. "When I went on the hunt with Papanick, we leave so fast I forget my grandfather's carved seal hunting charm. But now I am wearing it."

They had passed the second big bend in the Sitkin and were nearing the place where Mark had been leaving fish for the foxes. Kali could not be far away. Mark walked a little faster. He had waited five days for this moment, and now it was here and he was afraid. Kali might not come at his call.

"Why you go so fast, Mark?"

"We're coming to a place where—" Mark broke off suddenly at the sound of yapping foxes. It was the sassy yapping of young foxes at play. "That must be Kali!" cried Mark. "Come on!"

Dropping the sled rope, he went dashing across the ice toward the far bank. The river seemed wider than it ever had before. He hit a glassy-smooth patch near the shore and almost lost his rifle as his feet flew out from under him.

Oka laughed. The yapping of foxes grew louder and took on a frantic note. Just as Mark started up the bank through the tangle of ground willows he heard the angry, coughlike grunt of a large animal. An icy chill shot through him.

He took a firmer grip on his rifle. A moment later he reached the top. Two hundred yards away four white foxes were yipping at the heels of a lumbering polar bear.

11- alone in the night

MARK SAW at a glance that the foxes were enjoying themselves. They were playing a game with the polar bear. But they were young and foolish. If they came too close. . . .

The bear wheeled suddenly. Its huge paw

flashed out. Quick as the foxes were they barely escaped the slashing claws.

The attack seemed to be just what the foxes wanted. Their yipping grew shrill. They frolicked around the beast, darting in and out in a frenzy of reckless daring.

Oka suddenly caught his arm and drew him down. "That bear smart. See? He lead the foxes this way so he can get to the river. He like to fight better on the ice."

Mark sucked in his breath. Oka was right. The big polar bear was coming closer, angling toward the river in heavy, rocking-horse bounds, with the foxes yapping wildly at his heels.

"Will—will the bear kill them, Oka?"

"I don't know. Young foxes get excited, take too many chances."

Mark bit his lip. They didn't know much about slippery ice, either. His muscles tightened like stretched wire as he watched the great white beast put on a burst of speed as it neared the river. It was less than fifty yards upstream when it plunged down the steep embankment.

For an instant Mark thought the bear would turn at the bottom and get the foxes as they came flying down. But it didn't.

It hit the ice at a full gallop. Out on the river it

made for one of the slippery patches where the ice was as slick and smooth as a windowpane. And the crazy little foxes were right behind.

They were following too close!

Ice flew up in a spray as mighty claws dug in for a sudden stop. The bear spun. It reared.

Mark caught a glimpse of great open jaws. He heard the savage snarl. Then came the heavy crash of his gun as he squeezed the trigger.

The bear jerked back on its haunches. For an instant it sat stunned. A spot of red grew on its white chest. The bear began weaving its head back and forth, testing the air with its nose, trying to get their scent. It hadn't located them yet.

Mark reloaded.

"The head," whispered Oka. "Aim for the side of the head."

The polar bear reared suddenly to its full height. It saw them now. With a coughlike grunt it came streaking toward them across the ice.

"I make it turn," yelled Oka. He leaped to the tundra and ran along the edge, shouting to attract the bear's attention.

The bear turned to cut him off. Snow flew as it charged up the embankment. It was so close Mark could see the steamy puffs of its breath.

He fired.

The bear took a hard flop. It quivered. Like a limp bag of flesh it rolled slowly down the slope and came to rest on the ice. The foxes came rushing in to worry it again.

Mark slipped another cartridge into his rifle and stood ready. He had heard many stories of stunned bears that suddenly came back to life.

Oka came yelling, and pounded him on the back. "You got him, Mark! A big one! Your first polar bear. You shoot the first one in the village this year. Wait till the people see!"

Mark did not take his eyes from the bear. Things had happened so fast he wasn't quite sure about anything. "Didn't you shoot, Oka?" he asked.

"No. You killed by yourself. Bear belongs to you."

Together they went down the slope and advanced cautiously with their rifles ready. They made certain the bear was dead.

Mark lifted one of the huge paws. He felt weak and shivery when he thought what the sharp claws might have done to Kali.

Three of the foxes had drifted back to yap from a safe distance. The fourth, only ten yards away, was not yapping. It stood watching Mark curiously, its white head cocked to one side.

124

Mark nudged Oka. "Look at Kali," he whispered. "He never saw me dressed in winter furs before. He's not sure it's me."

Digging a small piece of fish from an inner pocket, Mark tossed it high. "Get it, Kali."

Kali sprang into the air. He caught it with a snap and gulped it down. Mark walked out and fed him the next piece out of his hand.

Mark glanced proudly at Oka. And suddenly he felt uneasy. Oka was glaring at him, his brows drawn down in a heavy scowl.

Pulling the supply sled, Mark continued up the river with only the foxes for company. Kali trotted beside him. Mark said, "I'm glad Oka went back to get someone to haul home the bear. It gives us a chance to be alone for a while."

He could hear the clicking of Kali's sharp claws on the ice. Kali's new winter coat was a spotless, gleaming white. He looked so light and airy that he seemed to float over the ice like a puff of frosty breath.

Mark paused to rest after an hour of steady going. One sharp whistle brought the foxes scooting back to him.

He chuckled. "When I whistle like that you know it means something good to eat."

He tossed bits of fish to the three, and fed Kali by hand. It thrilled him to see how quickly they had come to accept him again. But then they had known his voice and scent and whistle most of their lives; and he had fed them quite regularly up to a month ago. Kali pawed at him and nuzzled his hand for more fish.

"Not now." Mark picked up the sled rope again and started off. "We'll soon be at camp. Then you can have more. You kids got to get used to the place before Oka gets there. If you weren't so scared of him I think he'd like you, too."

Oka was going to be a problem. "I'll just have to be nice to him and please him as much as I can," Mark thought. "Then maybe he won't mind having the foxes around."

He broke into an easy trot. The foxes ranged ahead, moving like misty ghosts in the moonlight. He passed the gull cliffs, crumbling rock walls that rose straight up from the river on either side. Then the banks fell away again in slopes covered with ground willows and drifts of snow.

Mark kept a sharp eye on the left rim of the tundra. Presently he saw what he was looking for —the snow walls of the hunting-camp igloo. The igloo was perched just above the bank like a little fortress overlooking the river.

126

He drew up under it. With a shout to the foxes he left the sled on the ice and ran up the path. Everything seemed to be just as he and Oka had left it. There were four snow walls with a ridgepole in place, but no roof. Just inside the low entrance, in the right-hand corner, stood the camp stove, made from a five-gallon oil can. In the corner to the left stood their wooden grub box. It had a strong lid, for it contained a lantern, pots and pans, flour, sugar, tea, salt, and matches.

Moonlight came flooding down between the open walls. While Kali made an inspection of the place, Mark brought the packs up from the sled and collected willow-wood fuel along the cut of the river.

He covered the six-by-eight floor with two large caribou skins, placed fur-side down, and put two more on top, fur-side up. It made a double-layered rug which the cold could not penetrate. Next he brought in the sleeping bags and rolled them out, one on each side.

Kali, who had been watching with interest from the top of the snow wall, dropped down and began nosing back and forth, going over the furs like a busy vacuum cleaner. Mark's sleeping bag seemed to stir his memory. He dug his nose deep into the fur and sniffed eagerly.

127

"You ought to remember it," Mark said. "You slept on it enough."

He rolled the fox over on its back. It squirmed and kicked. But when Mark started rubbing its underside it lay perfectly still and half closed its eyes. Its dainty paws had thick pads of fur on the bottom, and black claws that were sharp as thorns.

He took off his mitten and ran his bare hand through the beautiful white fur. It felt silky, and as light and soft as the down of an eider duck's nest.

"You're a real snow fox now," he said, his soft voice filled with wonder. "I hope we can make Oka like you."

Mark slipped his mitten back on and stood up to stamp warmth back into his feet. Now that Kali felt at home it was time to put on the roof.

He spread a canvas over the ridgepole and the top of the walls, and weighed it down on both sides with blocks of snow so the wind would not blow it away. He put up a stovepipe, running it through a metal safety hole in the canvas roof. Crawling in through the low entrance, he lighted the lantern and hung it up by forcing the wire handle into the snow wall. Next he fixed a caribou skin over the entrance, then lighted the stove.

128

"There!" he said to Kali. "We'll soon have it warm now."

He was rather pleased with himself. It was the first time he had set up camp without Oka's help. Some day soon they were going to try to build a round snow igloo. None of his Eskimo friends had ever seen one except in their schoolbooks. According to the books, the round snow igloos were built by Greenland Eskimos.

Kali soon backed away from the stove. He sat watching it with keen interest, and listened to the crackling of the flames. The end of his tail began to twitch.

Mark took off his mitten and threw back his parka hood as the place became warm. It seemed to him that Oka should have been there by now. He remembered it was his turn to cook. He felt hungry already.

"If Oka doesn't get here pretty soon we're going to eat."

Kali whined. His beautiful bushy tail began sweeping slowly back and forth, the way it always did when he was unhappy about something. Suddenly the heat became too much for him. He made a dash for the door and slipped out.

Mark fed the foxes enough fish to keep them

from wandering off in search of food. He spent the next half hour melting snow for drinking water. The light snow on top of the drifts was not very good for that because it held so little water. He dug deep into a drift to get the coarse, icy-grained snow near the bottom and melted enough to fill the two-quart can at the back of the stove.

He couldn't imagine what was keeping Oka. Time passed slowly without Kali to keep him company. Outside, the stillness of the arctic night was broken now and then by the howling of wolves in the distance.

All at once the foxes began yapping. Mark smiled, for he knew it meant Oka was coming at last. The foxes made good watchdogs.

Mark started preparing their evening meal. There wasn't much to do. He had already cooked it at home, a mixture of baked beans and bits of stewed caribou meat. While it was still hot he had poured it out thin on a canvas and allowed it to freeze. The frozen dinner had then been broken into chunks that looked a little like peanut brittle, and stored in a canvas bag. All he had to do now was pour the frozen chunks into a pan and melt them down on the stove.

In a few minutes the igloo was filled with the savory odors of baked beans and stewed caribou meat. Dinner was ready. But Oka, for some strange reason, had not yet arrived.

Mark suddenly became alarmed as he realized he had not heard the foxes for several minutes. That didn't make sense. They should have been yapping all the while as Oka came nearer.

Taking the pot off the stove he went out to investigate. From the rim of the tundra he could look down the river nearly as far as the gull cliffs, where the channel turned and moonlight shone on the ice like shavings of silver. Oka was not in sight.

He called Kali. If any of the foxes were near they were standing so still he couldn't see them against the snow. Somewhere among the willows a tundra chicken cackled like a barnyard hen with a sore throat. Mark gave a sharp whistle and waited. But the foxes did not come.

Silence thickened about him. The vast white wilderness of ice and snow lay empty and lifeless. Nothing stirred. Nothing moved at all except the frosty clouds of his breath.

Something had disturbed the foxes. Someone, man or beast, had come close enough to excite them.

It was probably some animal, he decided. The playful foxes would take after almost any animal that came along and give it a good chase.

There was really nothing to worry about, he told himself. But he was alone in the night, and that was not a good feeling to have when the village and safety were miles away.

He looked at the tundra beyond the river. Had the people over there spotted his camp? Were they watching him now? He wondered what they might do if they knew he was all alone.

He moved his rifle a few inches closer to the door, where he could reach out and grab it at a moment's notice. Guns could not be taken into heated places, for then moisture would form on the cold metal and the rifle would freeze up and be useless when it was taken out into the cold again.

After one last fearful glance across the river, he ducked into the igloo. He took a seat right next to the door flap and waited, his ears straining for the slightest sound.

As time passed he became more and more anxious about Oka. Something had happened to him. He might have fallen on the ice and broken a leg, or a bear might have cornered him. Those people across the river might have. . . .

132

Mark suddenly stiffened. He could hear the creaking sounds of footsteps in the snow. Someone was coming. The sounds grew louder.

Then came Oka's familiar voice. "Hey, Mark! You in there?"

Shuddering with relief Mark whipped the door flap aside. "Come on!"

He placed the dinner back on the stove and quickly struggled out of his parka. He did not want Oka to know how worried he had been.

Oka came in on hands and knees, wearing a broad grin. But there was a strange tightness in his face. Mark knew better than to ask questions. Something had happened, and Oka would tell him about it in his own good time if he felt like it.

The beans and stewed meat were soon simmering again. While they ate, Oka kept up a lively chatter about the excitement in the village when he had come with news about the polar bear.

"Your father so proud he can't say anything," said Oka. "Everybody remember how good aim you have and how fast you can shoot. Your father want to skin the bear himself."

Mark grinned. Killing the bear had not seemed very important at the time, but maybe it really was. His father and the Eskimos thought so. He had a warm feeling for all of them suddenly. It was going to be fun to go home and hear what they had to say.

For dessert, Oka surprised him by digging the leg bones of a large caribou out of his pack. The bones were uncooked, and had bits of raw meat and tufts of hair still clinging to them. But Mark did not mind. He knew the goodness that lay within.

Using the back of his knife he cracked the bone with a sharp blow. Out came a creamy white plug of frozen marrow, which he licked and sucked and chewed on as though it were a lollipop. But it tasted much better than a lollipop. It was as smooth and cold as ice cream on his tongue, and had a delicious nutty flavor.

"Are these bones from the caribou you shot?" he asked.

"It was only a small thin cow," said Oka modestly. "And so lame I could have run up and caught it by the tail."

Mark knew better. Eskimos always said things like that so no one would think they were boasting.

Flashing a wide smile, Oka said, "Tomorrow night we have a big feast of leg bones, I think. We hunt all day, kill plenty caribou."

He reached for the leather thong at his throat, and drawing out his charm bag, produced an old ivory carving of a seal. "You see? My grand-father's most powerful hunting charm. The spirit of the seals brings us good luck when we wear this because we were once the Seal People."

Mark remembered the ivory carving he carried in his charm bag. "I found an ivory carving on the beach last summer," he said.

"A seal carving like this?"

"No. It was a carving of a sitting fox."

"No, not a fox," said Oka, laughing. "Maybe it so old and used up it look like a fox. A fox carving no good for charm. It would bring bad luck."

Mark was about to take it out and show it to him. But he changed his mind. Oka still seemed disturbed about something that must have happened on his way to camp. If he knew a fox carving was right here in camp he might get the idea it was bringing them bad luck.

Mark kept listening for the foxes. Kali was so used to running wild and free on the tundra that he might forget to come back.

"The foxes followed me all the way to camp," he told Oka. "A little while ago I heard them yapping at something, but when I went out they were gone. I'll bet they went chasing after another bear."

"Not a bear," said Oka quietly.

135

"How do you know?"

Oka picked up pieces of bone he had dropped. "I know because they saw same thing I saw. When I come up river I hear yapping like you and me hear before. So I think they chase another bear. I climb up the bank to look."

"What was it?"

The tightness came back into Oka's face. "Dog sleds. Three dog sleds. More of those people coming down from mountains. I started walking again and I find place where sleds leave river and go up bank. At that place I see tracks of five sleds in the snow."

Mark stared. "What do you think it means?"

Oka did not answer. He began picking up pieces of bone again, as though he had said all he meant to say.

Mark became impatient. He was tired of Eskimo mysteries. "You know lots about those people you never tell me," he complained. "I know more than you think. Texas Andy told us the whole story, even about Tornick, the witch doctor. Maybe he's coming back now to get revenge."

"There are many people over there this winter. Always watching. I think myself many of our

136

hunters come back quick from the caribou hunt because they worry. But no one say that."

"What are those people over there watching for, Oka?" asked Mark. "They don't need more guards for their hunting grounds this year. No one ever goes hunting on their land."

"Joseph thinks they are watching for something else." Oka crawled over to the door and threw out the broken bones. "Many times our hunters see the watchers looking over at this side of the river. They never do that before."

Mark shot an uneasy glance toward the entrance. He wished now they hadn't built their igloo so close to the river. In a tight voice he said, "If they were planning to attack, they might want to study us and see how many hunters we have. Do you think we should go home and tell about those five sleds?"

Oka wrinkled his nose, meaning "no." "Our people watching, too. If we go home now everybody say we are afraid. We help more by hunting the caribou."

12- the caribou hunt

THEY HAD traveled upriver for more than an hour early the next morning, when Oka stopped to examine some caribou tracks. The morning was cold and clear. Stars glittered like frost in the immense and lonely sky.

"Two, maybe three herds cross river here," announced Oka. "Some tracks real fresh, only a few hours old. If I follow, maybe I find where herd is resting."

138

"You don't want me to go along?"

Oka looked down at the tracks. "One hunter is more quiet than two."

Mark knew Oka was thinking about the noisy foxes, who were yapping and chasing tundra chickens up ahead. "All right," he said, trying not to sound pleased. "You follow the tracks and I'll just go up the river a ways."

"Don't go too far. I make big circle. If I can't get close enough to shoot, maybe I scare some back this way. Put on your snow shirt if you see caribou."

"I will," promised Mark.

"I think I put mine on right away," said Oka. He took his snow shirt out of his knapsack. Made of white canvas, it slipped on over his furs like a long nightgown and made him almost invisible against the snow.

Oka climbed the bank. With a parting wave he disappeared over the rim of the tundra.

Shifting his knapsack, Mark continued on up the river, moving quietly over the naked ice. For a long time he could hear the loud shrieking of snow under Oka's feet. Once in a while the ice boomed, or the tundra cracked with a loud report.

Up ahead somewhere, but not in sight, the foxes

were yapping. Mark whistled for them. In two yips and a yap they were there, bouncing about him like silvery wraiths in the moonlight. He gave them each a bit of fish. They made enough noise for ten foxes.

"It's a good thing Oka isn't here now," Mark thought. He didn't blame Oka. "If I really wanted to go hunting, I'd know better than to take a noisy pack of foxes along. But Oka knows hunting is poor now. He just likes to hunt. It's fun for him, just like it's fun for me to be with the foxes."

The moon, which had been wandering around among the stars for over a week without setting, now hung low in the western sky. Slanting blue shadows darkened the cut of the river.

Tundra chickens were cackling in a ravine thick with willows. As the foxes swung in to stalk them, the lookout bird of the flock, perched on a branch like a clump of snow, suddenly came to life. With a loud squawk the white birds rocketed up and whipped out of sight over the bench of the tundra. So perfectly did they match the snow that Mark saw only the flash of their black tail feathers.

To play a trick on Kali he ran up the river a ways

and hid behind a large boulder. He waited for several minutes. The foxes weren't yapping now. They had probably continued up the ravine in search of tundra chickens and rabbits.

Just below his hiding place a thin drift of snow swung out over the ice. There were sled tracks across it, probably tracks made by the sleds Oka had seen. Or had more sleds come during the night? Mark shot a glance up the river, half expecting to see more sleds coming around the bend. If more were on the way they would swing into sight without warning, coming so suddenly he wouldn't have a chance to hide.

But he had his rifle. He wouldn't be helpless. They wouldn't come very close with their bows and arrows when they saw he was well armed.

A cold, prickly sensation passed over him suddenly as a small piece of crusted snow came tumbling down the embankment. It stopped only inches away from where he was crouching behind the rock. He glanced up at the rim of the tundra above, and found himself face to face with a strange Eskimo.

All he could see was the Eskimo's head. The Eskimo was lying down in the snow. The face was

141

young, that of a boy; and the boy seemed just as surprised as he did. For a breathless moment they looked at each other.

While Mark was trying to collect his wits he saw a change come over the face. Timidly at first, the boy grinned down at him. The grin grew until the whole face was a part of it.

The boy let out a squeaky giggle. Mark smiled. The boy laughed. Suddenly they were both laughing.

Mark had the good warm feeling of one who has

just made a wonderful discovery. These people weren't enemies. They were friends!

But a moment later he wasn't so sure. Without warning the boy's head disappeared. The boy could not have moved back so quickly by himself. Someone else was up there, and that someone must have dragged the boy back with a powerful jerk.

Backing slowly away Mark kept his eyes on the snowy rim. He thought he heard angry whispers. He walked swiftly downstream to get away from the place.

What strange people they were. They went to no end of trouble to watch others, but they did not want to be seen themselves. Why?

Hurrying back to the ravine he turned in to look for the foxes. He could neither see nor hear them. Their trail led deeper into the ravine, over snow-drifts and through thick patches of willow, then up the steep side and onto the tundra. He followed it. The moment he raised his head above the tundra he saw them. They were scattered, trotting back and forth over a large area swept almost clean of snow.

They were hunting lemmings, the furry little tundra mice whose runway tunnels ran everywhere under the frozen grass. Every once in a while a fox stopped and cocked its head as if it were listening. Then it leaped straight up in the air and came down with its nose and feet all bunched together. It usually caught the mouse under its sharp claws, and ate it on the spot. When the foxes were no longer hungry, they buried their mice in the snow where they could come back to them later.

Far off to the left, above the horizon, northern lights shot wavering fingers of blue and gold, green and old rose, high into the heavens. It was as if giant searchlights from another world were sweeping their beams across the sky.

As Mark watched, the lights grew in brilliance until the whole sky was aglow with rippling banners. Kali came up to nuzzle his face. The little fox shook itself, and thousands of bits of frost, flying from its coat, formed a flash rainbow over its back.

Kali went off again to join in the hunt. Just as he caught a lemming a great snowy owl came out of nowhere to swoop down at him. Kali flattened against the ground.

The bird passed over him and Kali dashed for the nearest snowbank with the mouse in his jaws. The owl swooped again. Its sharp talons narrowly missed his face. But Kali seemed to know the bird was only after his mouse. He buried it safely in the snow. When the owl dived again he leaped at it with an angry yip.

Dawn brightened the southern sky. The northern lights faded out. So did the stars. Presently the whole sweep of the tundra lay in soft pearly light. Mark knew it was about eleven o'clock in the morning. He put on his sunglasses.

Now in December the sun no longer came up over the horizon. He would not see it again for two whole months. But the arctic night was not nearly so dark as he had once believed, for there was twilight every day for about two hours. Arctic nights were usually bright and clear. Even when there was no moon the stars and the northern lights brightened the sky and sparkled in the snow.

The coming of dawn reminded Mark that he hadn't eaten for several hours. He slipped back into the ravine and stamped his feet and swung his arms briskly until the stiffness was gone, and he felt all loose and warm again.

Sitting down he took a frozen fish from his pack. With his hunting knife he shaved off thin slices no larger than potato chips and popped them into his mouth. It was raw fish, the typical lunch of the Eskimo hunter. But it tasted neither raw nor fishy. He chewed the chips and enjoyed their delicate flavor.

He heard the creaking of snow in the distance. The sounds grew louder and louder as he ate. A large number of men or animals was coming toward him over the snow. Oka had probably managed to chase a herd of caribou back toward the river. Not that it mattered much. When wolves were about, anything that moved could frighten caribou. Their eyesight was so poor they were certain to mistake the foxes for wolves and take to their heels.

"I wouldn't have a chance to shoot even if I wanted to," he told himself.

But a herd of caribou, moving under a nodding forest of tall antlers, was a sight worth seeing. Mark climbed eagerly to his perch at the edge of the tundra. Sounds seemed to be coming from all sides. In the east, the direction Oka had taken, he could make out the dark line of a moving caribou herd that seemed to be floating between sky and earth.

The arctic twilight was playing tricks again. It had wiped out all the shadows of the tundra. Even the horizons had disappeared, for snow and sky

146

were all one vast misty brightness without beginning or end.

Nothing seemed real. The caribou seemed to be coming right out of the sky. They were coming fast. The herd came on like a dark surging tide. Mark guessed there were several hundred of them. He could soon hear the odd clicking and snapping and popping sounds made by their loose ankle joints.

He glanced at the foxes. They had given up mouse hunting and were now sitting on the tops of boulders like so many owls, for they too were watching the oncoming herd.

All at once Kali let out a string of shrill hunting barks. The others joined in the challenge. The four leaped from their rocks and went racing toward the herd in a noisy charge.

The caribou suddenly stopped in their tracks. They remained motionless, poised for instant flight, heads erect, antlers towering majestically against the sky. They stared at the charging foxes.

For Mark it was a thrilling and breathless moment. He kept his eyes on the cow in the lead. One toss of her head, one snort of alarm, was all it would take to set the herd off at a flying gallop. But moments passed and nothing of the sort happened.

147

The cow leader continued her staring until the saucy foxes were yapping and dancing right under her nose.

They were trying to tease her into a charge. They wanted to play as they had played with the bear. But the cow would not charge. She merely stood there gazing down at them.

The foxes turned to other animals in the herd. A young bull rushed at them. That was what they wanted. They worried him into one wild charge after another.

As he watched, Mark saw a remarkable change come over the herd. The animals were spreading out. They were pawing away snow to get at the mosses and lichens beneath. The whole herd was calmly beginning to feed! Somehow the foxes had brought about the change.

Mark suddenly felt a quiver of excitement as he realized the importance of his discovery. The caribou clearly felt safer when foxes were near. They seemed to know foxes feared wolves as much as they did and would not be about if wolves were near. They seemed to know that foxes, with their much keener senses, would warn them of approaching danger long before they could sense the danger themselves.

Mark slid back down the embankment several feet to get out of sight. Fumbling in his pack he drew out his white canvas snow shirt and slipped it on over his furs.

Texas Andy had been wrong! He had said there was nothing foxes could do that dogs couldn't do better. But that wasn't true. Dogs were useless for hunting caribou. They always frightened the herd away. But foxes! Why, they were just what caribou hunters needed. They could calm a whole herd and make the big deer feel so safe that hunters could easily get within range and shoot as many as they needed.

Kali wasn't useless. He wasn't just a plaything, a toy, as the Eskimos seemed to think. But Mark knew no one would believe that unless he brought home caribou meat to prove it.

His heart thumped as he picked up his rifle. "I'll have to shoot a couple," he said grimly, clamping his jaw hard. "Then they'll have to believe. They'll see what Kali can do. Even Oka will be glad to have him along after this."

He edged up into firing position, with his head and shoulders just above the level of the tundra. Twice he took careful aim and squeezed the trigger.

Two animals were down. The rest calmly continued feeding. The reports of his rifle had not frightened them at all, for the shots sounded like the loud cracking noises constantly coming from the frozen tundra.

The caribou yearlings and foxes were still playing their game of tag. They dashed in and out of the feeding herd, and sometimes ran around some old bull or cow that paid no attention to them at all.

What a pity it was that the Eskimo hunters weren't there. They would gladly have come many miles and suffered many hardships for a chance at a herd like this. They had their families to feed through the winter. Their ice cellars were almost empty. Some were already so desperate for food they were eating the fish set aside for their dogs. Though the best seal hunting came in the spring, many Eskimos had been forced to go out on the ice much earlier than usual.

Mark looked at the caribou feeding so peacefully. He had been willing to kill for the sake of Kali. But what about the Eskimos? They were his people. They were proud of him for having killed the polar bear. Now they needed his help. If he let the herd go, many of his friends would be hungry this winter. They'd have to suffer because of his weakness.

Mark swallowed. A hot wave of shame passed over him.

Setting his lips firmly, he reloaded his gun. He knew exactly where his bullets had to strike the ribs so the animals would lie down quietly and not frighten the rest of the herd. A shot in the shoulder might cause an animal to jump, and it would spoil good shoulder meat.

He shot only the cows, for they were fat and sleek at this time of the year. The bulls were now thin. They were easy to spot and avoid, since they had lost their antlers a few weeks ago after the mating season.

The thick winter coats were too heavy for clothing, but could be used for rugs and blankets. Some of the hides, with the fur scraped off, would be used to make leather harnesses for the dogs, and leather pouches and thongs. From the sinews the Eskimo women would make sewing thread, and snares with which to catch rabbits and tundra chickens. The marrow of the leg bones, beaten in large bowls and mixed with berries and bits of prunes, would make delicious, creamy white Eskimo ice cream.

He went over these things in his mind as he fired shot after shot. He was bringing health and happiness to his people. Hunting was work, the most important work that a man of the North could do. He kept at it until he had used up the last of his ammunition.

Even then he was careful not to frighten the herd. Oka could not be very far away. He was probably crawling up to get within shooting range at that very moment.

Mark ducked out of sight. Just as he turned to go down the embankment he saw the crouching figures below. He jerked back with a start.

13- taken prisoner

THE STRANGE Eskimos crouching below were watching him. Their eyes were like spear points and arrows. For a long moment of terror Mark froze. He couldn't move. His heart hammered wildly against his ribs.

What were they doing on this side of the river? Why were they staring? What did they want?

Then, like an unreal monster rising out of a nightmare, one of them slowly straightened up and started toward him. He came on, one slow step at a time. The others were rising now in the same slow way.

Mark suddenly came to life. With all his strength he flung his empty rifle at the nearest. Their shouts rang in his ears as he spun and started up, thrashing and clawing over the shelf of loose snow.

Wild snorts of alarm came from the caribou. They saw him and were off in a flash.

Just as he gained the tundra someone grabbed his foot. He was jerked back. Then he was rolling head over heels down the slope in a tangle of arms and legs.

At the bottom he lay stunned, his face pressed in the snow. He guessed three or four were holding him down. They were all talking at once in excited, jabbering voices. But he had no idea what they were saying.

One of them shouted. From a distance came answering shouts that sounded like cheers. He felt them tugging at his fur boots. They were taking them off. Sick with fear he wondered if they were planning some horrible kind of torture. There was no telling what uncivilized savages might do.

The cold air felt like ice on his naked feet. He tried to kick, but they held his ankles firmly. Then, for no reason that he could think of, their voices rose to a feverish pitch of excitement.

Moments later they put on his boots again. He was lifted to his feet and led down the ravine to the river. On the river ice a waiting crowd of Eskimos stared as if he were someone from another planet.

There were quick questions and answers. One of his guards kept pointing to the tundra and to Mark's feet, explaining something over and over again in an angry voice. A few seemed cheered by what they heard. But most stared in silence and looked troubled.

It was plain that they had just arrived from the

mountains. There were at least a dozen dog sleds on the ice, all facing downriver. The frost-covered dogs were breathing hard and looked as though they had been driven without mercy for many hours. It surprised him to find that most of the hunters were armed with rifles.

A group of them left the crowd and ran into the ravine and on up over the lip of the tundra. Mark suddenly realized what they were up to. They were going to help themselves to the meat and hides of his caribou, the caribou he had shot for the village.

Anger burned hot in his cheeks. He wanted to break loose and fight them all. He wanted to scream that they were low-down thieves. But his fear was stronger than his anger. He pressed his lips tightly together and tried to hide his feelings. Never before in his life had he felt so utterly helpless.

Several other dog sleds arrived, and the crowd about him grew larger and larger. They were becoming uneasy. They kept glancing upriver as if waiting for someone.

There could be only one person that important —a witch doctor. Ordinary Eskimo tribes were not ruled by chiefs or leaders. A cold shudder ran up Mark's back as he wondered if the mad witch doctor, Tornick, were still alive.

Presently the Eskimos tired of waiting. They unloaded one of the sleds and made him sit down on it. His guards ran on each side as the dogs followed the river far below the gull cliffs and then swung up the embankment and headed west across the snow-covered barrens.

Less than a mile from the river, where the tundra dipped beyond a jumble of rocks, they entered a village of dome-shaped tents made of caribou skins.

Women and children came running to look at him. There were more questions and answers. One of the guards lifted a bearskin hanging over a door. Mark was taken into the cavelike dimness where licking flames leaped a foot high from a stone bowl, an old-fashioned Eskimo oil lamp.

The women crowded in after him. They drew off his fur boots and examined his feet in wonder. They seemed excited and happy and angry at the same time; and haunted looks crept into their faces. They left quickly.

Then Mark found himself alone, except for two guards who sat near the door. The oil lamp began to flicker unevenly. One of the guards straightened the long cotton wick and dropped a piece of blubber into the bowl. When the blubber melted and became oil, the flame brightened again. Its wavering light played over the framework of mountain willow branches supporting the tent.

Hours passed. They were endless hours of waiting. Now and then one of the guards crawled out, only to return a few moments later, plainly disappointed about something. Eskimos usually had great patience, but these two seemed anxious and uneasy.

To Mark it seemed like a bad dream from which he must soon awaken. None of it made sense. He could not imagine why his feet had stirred so much excitement and anger.

It wasn't likely that anything would happen to him until their leader arrived. But if their leader turned out to be Tornick, the mad witch doctor, he could expect no mercy. Tornick would hardly come such a long way in the winter unless he meant to attack the village and reap his terrible revenge.

It suddenly dawned on Mark that the war had started already. They had captured him and were holding him prisoner. They had stolen his caribou. What were these if not acts of war? They were proof that Tornick was still alive.

Mark's throat tightened until it hurt as he

159

thought of his parents and Milly and all his Eskimo friends. What would happen to them? They would not be taken by surprise, but they would be outnumbered and probably did not know their enemies were armed with rifles.

A fresh wave of hopelessness passed over him. There was nothing he could do.

Time dragged on. Once again the flame in the stone lamp began to flutter. It was a long time before the guards took notice of it. They were becoming more and more careless as their restlessness grew. There were times, he noticed, when they seemed to forget about him completely.

A tiny spark of hope began burning within him. If he could escape, if he could make it back to the village, it might upset their plan of attack. They would then know they could no longer hope to take the village by surprise. If they were nearly as superstitious as old-fashioned Eskimos were supposed to be, they would probably take his escape as a warning that their spirit gods were against them. That would be enough to make them call off the war and head right back for their mountains.

He glanced at the caribou-skin wall behind him and suddenly remembered his hunting knife.

160

With one slash he could cut his way through and make a run for it. He was quite sure one of the guards had a gun just outside the tent. But with luck and a burst of speed he could be off to a good start, and in his white snow shirt he would not be an easy target.

The beating of his heart quickened as he inched back to the wall. Just as he reached for his hunting knife a guard moved. He stiffened. In the uncertain light it seemed to him that the guard was watching out of the corner of an eye. But he couldn't be sure.

For several tense minutes he remained perfectly still, not daring to move a muscle. Cold sweat broke out on his face. His breath sounded loud and harsh in his tight throat.

Presently the tension was broken by distant sounds. The guards turned to the door. One crawled out. The other held back the bearskin flap so that he could look out.

Cold arctic air came pouring along the floor like an icy flood. Mark shivered. The creaking of snow and clamor of voices and howling of dogs told him a large party was rapidly approaching the tent village.

His time was running out. But it was a perfect moment to make an escape. In the noise and confusion he might even be able to slip away unnoticed. He lifted the bottom of his snow shirt and reached for his knife. His fingers found the leather sheath. It was limp and empty. His knife was gone.

Now the party was entering the village. Turning, Mark caught the bottom edge of the tent wall and tugged frantically to lift it enough so that he could slip under. But the skin wall was solidly frozen to snow which had been banked around the outside. It couldn't be budged.

A sob caught in Mark's throat as he gave up. He had done his best and failed. He fell back, weak and breathless, against a roll of caribou blankets, and closed his eyes to shut out the sight of his tent prison.

Sounds and voices were coming from every direction now. The village was crowded with people and dogs sleds, and he felt sure that Tornick was there among them.

Someone entered and came close to him. A voice said, "Mark!"

He sat up with a start. In front of him sat an Eskimo boy his own age. It was the boy who had laughed from the rim of the tundra. The boy smiled. Once again Mark felt the friendliness of that smile.

He wondered if the boy understood the simple language Eskimos used when they spoke to white people. Trying it, he said, "How do you know my name?"

The boy smiled even broader. "I am Terigan. I live here. In all my life I never saw the mountains. I keep watch of our hunting grounds with my father and uncles. Many times I heard your friends call you Mark."

The boy seemed friendly. But how could he be a friend when he belonged to the enemy tribe? Mark eyed him with suspicion. "Did you come here to look at my feet?" he asked.

"I saw them once when you walked on the wet sand. I know they are not like the feet of caribou."

"Caribou! Why should I have feet like that?"

Terigan lost his smile. "Tornick told us. He told us always to stay away from white people. He said they belonged to the bad spirits and had feet like caribou. But now everybody knows Tornick lied. The people are angry."

So that was it! Tornick had to tell lies to keep his tribe from having anything to do with whites.

Even their rifles must have been bought from wandering Indian and Eskimo tribes.

"But your people have seen the feet of a white man before," said Mark. "Many years ago a white trading-post man from our village went out on the cape and never came back. Your tribe must have killed him."

Terigan seemed surprised. He turned and questioned the guard.

The guard spoke to Mark in the simple language. "There was a man who came out to dig in the old caves near the village of the dead many years ago. He was killed by a falling rock. Animals fed on him. We found a few bones and torn clothing."

Terigan smiled again. Shyly he held out a black-feathered arrow. "Remember the time you saw one like this?"

Someone lifted the bearskin just then and spoke to the guards. Terigan looked frightened. "Tornick has sent for you," he whispered.

Mark felt a chill go through him. His stomach tightened into knots as the guards took him out. The tent village was crowded with Eskimos. They watched him in silence. As he walked through the crowd with his guards his legs began to tremble and give way at the knees.

164

14- Tornick

THEY TOOK him into a large tent, which was crowded with hunters, and brought him before the leaping flames of two stone oil lamps. Between the lamps, seated on cushions of fur, was the oldest man he had ever seen.

Tornick sat as motionless as a statue, a parka hood framing his skull-like face. The sunken mouth was all wrinkles running together. Deep-set eyes stared out at him from shadowy sockets.

Mark shrank back. He had heard many horrible things about witch doctors and their strange powers. He had laid all that to Eskimo superstitions. But somehow this creature did not seem human.

No one made a sound. Tornick said nothing. He did not move. Seconds passed, and minutes. Mark stood there staring at the shadowy eye sockets.

Something was happening to him. He didn't know what. But it was happening. He couldn't look away.

Some evil force seemed to be closing around him like an invisible cloud of smothering heat. His skin crawled. In all that time Tornick did not move so much as a muscle. He did not even seem to be breathing.

There wasn't a sound to be heard. The silence became so complete that it made a high-pitched ringing in his ears. The ringing became a steady hum, and the hum grew louder and louder, until the whole tent was filled with sound.

Tornick's face began to blur and waver before his eyes. His eyelids grew heavy and wanted to close.

166

He was fighting to keep them open when loud coughing startled him. Someone close by was seized with a terrible fit of coughing.

Mark turned to look at the one who was coughing. The dizzy, underwater feeling passed away instantly. He could see clearly again, and was surprised to find that everyone else, even his guards, was seated on the floor. He stood alone in the center of the tent. The eyes of all were upon him. Why? What were they expecting to see?

He knew only that some kind of struggle had taken place between himself and Tornick. In some mysterious way Tornick had tried to cast a spell over him. If the witch doctor was trying to prove that his magic was powerful even against a white person, he had failed already, but only because someone had happened to cough at the right moment.

An Eskimo stood up and began speaking to the witch doctor, pointing now and then to Mark. Others stood up and spoke. They seemed to be explaining something at great length. Finally Tornick replied in a thin, rasping voice.

His words brought shouts and angry cries from the men. Many leaped to their feet. They all tried to be heard at once. Everyone seemed greatly alarmed and very much against what the witch doctor had said.

Tornick alone remained calm. His face was like an evil mask. As he turned slightly his sunken eyes caught the lamplight and gleamed like red embers of a driftwood fire.

All at once Tornick had heard enough. He put a stop to their talk by grunting a sharp command.

For a moment the men stood as if stunned. Slowly they took their seats again, their faces dark with helpless rage. It gave Mark shivers to see how completely the mad witch doctor had them in his power.

A great sighing came from the crowd outside the tent. Several women began wailing softly.

Mark swayed on his feet. He tried to steady himself. He told himself he wasn't afraid. But he felt certain the wails of the women could mean only one thing—the swift coming of death.

Then Tornick spoke again, nodding to a big moon-faced Eskimo.

The man rose. He came to Mark and said in the simple language, "Many have seen you run on the tundra with the wild foxes. We have seen how you talk to them and play with them."

168

One of the seated guards plucked at Mark's sleeve. "I myself, and many with me, saw how the foxes helped when you hunted caribou. They are your brothers. When you call they come to you."

"It is true," said the moon-faced one. "All this we have told Tornick. Now he has asked that you bring him one of your foxes."

Mark eyed the man in silence. It took him a moment to realize that he had not been sentenced to die. They had been talking about the foxes all the while!

"Call a fox for Tornick," demanded the moon-faced one. "When you give it to him he will know that our words are true."

Mark stood there, not knowing what to do. What difference did it make whether Tornick believed or not? Why should a fox suddenly be so important? Questions buzzed in his mind like hungry tundra mosquitoes.

The moon-faced one pointed to the door. "Go! Go quickly to the river and call the foxes."

Mark glanced back at his guard. They were still seated and seemed to be in no hurry to take him out.

"We have seen that the foxes do not come close unless you are alone," explained the moon-faced one. "We will all wait for you here. Go!"

169

The man seemed to mean what he said. Dazed, Mark slowly went to the door and crawled out. A large group of Eskimos crowded about the entrance. They silently made way for him.

It was crazy. It wasn't real. It wasn't happening at all. Yet the Eskimos seemed real. He saw their faces clearly in the moonlight as he passed. They looked frightened. They watched his going as if they knew some terrible thing was about to happen. A woman sitting in the snow beyond the crowd rocked back and forth, wailing a sad lament.

"Listen for the voice," she cried as he passed. "Listen well for the voice of the spirit."

Then the village and people and the jumble of boulders were behind him. There was nothing ahead but the broad white sweep of the open tundra. He ran. He was free. He could go home again. He ran until his wind gave out and the village of tents was far behind him.

He glanced back. He wasn't being followed. The people were now watching him from the boulders. But they were too far behind to catch up with him now. He slowed down to a walk.

Northern lights shimmered faintly overhead. It wasn't nearly so cold as it had been for several days. Far to the east clouds darkened the sky.

170

Suddenly, from the cluster of domed tents behind him came quavering sing-song howls and wild whoops and drumbeats, and something that sounded like the yapping of foxes. The unearthly din made the tent village seem much closer than it really was.

Mark broke into a run again. The panicky feeling came back. It wasn't natural that Tornick should have let him go. Tornick was up to one of his tricks. Something was wrong.

15- voice of the spirit

DID THE mad witch doctor really expect him to bring back a fox?

"I didn't promise anything," Mark told himself. "They all knew I'd try to escape if I had a chance."

He reached the river, plunged down the embankment and headed downstream for the village.

"Mark!" An Eskimo stepped from behind a boulder. It was young Terigan. "You go the wrong way. The foxes are up at your camping place."

Mark stopped short. "W-what are you doing here?" he stammered. He saw the bow in the boy's hand. "Tornick—he sent you to guard me."

"Nobody knows I am here," replied Terigan. "I listened outside Tornick's tent. I heard what they said. I ran here fast so you wouldn't go home."

172

Mark stared helplessly at the bow. It was a powerful weapon. "You mean I'm your prisoner? You'll shoot if I run?"

Terigan studied the bank of the river a moment and pointed to a snow-capped bird's nest in the fork of a willow. "See the nest?"

All in an instant he reached for an arrow, drew, and let fly. Snow and grass exploded from the willow branch.

"Fast like that I killed the wolf to save the baby fox," Terigan said. He held up an arrow. "See? My arrows have the black feathers. But my father was angry with me for shooting the wolf. He said I might have frightened you so much that you would never come back again to run with the wild foxes."

Mark took a step back, and another. "Why should your father be angry? Why should he want me to play on your side of the river?"

"Because my father had already sent a message back to the mountains telling our people to come see you run with the wild foxes. He told them it was a very good sign."

It sounded like crazy talk. Yet the boy seemed very serious. "A good sign?" asked Mark. "What does he mean by that?"

Terigan moved closer. He seemed to forget that

Mark was his prisoner. "My father said you could not be such a good friend of the foxes if the spirit of wild foxes did not like you. That is why it is a good sign. You are a friend of the spirit."

"I am?" asked Mark, trying to keep up the conversation. The boy had dropped his guard now and was leaning carelessly on his bow. Mark stepped a little closer. "You mean all your people came from the mountains just to see me run with the foxes?"

"They all came to see you. Some came early. They had to watch many days before they saw you run with the foxes."

Mark edged closer still. Suddenly he sprang. His shoulder struck the boy hard in the chest. They went down together. Grunting and gasping, they struggled back and forth over the ice. They rolled over and over. The boy suddenly lost his grip on his bow. That was all Mark wanted.

He fought his way to the top, tore loose from the boy, and leaped to his feet. He picked up the bow. Threatening to use it as a club, he backed slowly away.

"You lie!" he gasped. "You tell many lies. I know why your people are here. Tornick brought them down to attack our village."

The boy slowly sat up. He looked at Mark soberly and rubbed the back of his neck.

Still backing away, Mark said, "If your people came here to watch me they wouldn't want to catch me and hold me prisoner."

"My people watched you shoot caribou. They saw how the foxes helped you. They caught you to see your feet," said Terigan as he rose from the ice. "If you had feet like the caribou they would know you belonged to the bad spirits and could not be a true friend to the spirit of wild foxes. When they saw you had feet like ours they held you to show Tornick."

"Tornick didn't see my feet," said Mark. He started away at a swift trot, once again heading for home.

"Wait!" yelled Terigan. "Listen for the voice of the spirit. The spirit of wild foxes will tell you not to go home."

Mark glanced back over his shoulder. The boy was following a few yards behind. He ran faster.

"If you go home they will know you are not a friend of the spirit," shouted the boy. "It will be a bad sign. Then Tornick will lead us to fight against your village. Many will die. The spirit will tell you I speak the truth."

175

Mark tried not to listen.   He was not going to be tricked again.   Lengthening his stride, he ran even faster.   But the young Eskimo would not give up.

"Hear the drums," he cried.   "Tornick is dancing to please the spirit.   Tornick is afraid of you. He wants you to go home so he can make war on the Seal People."

Slipping and sliding across a slick patch of ice, Mark kept going.

"Tornick is dancing hard so the spirit will stay to watch him and forget all about you," cried Terigan.   "Tornick is trying to keep the spirit away from you.   He is afraid the spirit will warn you not to go home."

Mark slowed down.   Could the boy be telling the truth?   Was Tornick trying to start a war by tricking him into going home?   It seemed too crazy to believe.   Yet the mad witch doctor must have had some evil reason for allowing him to escape.

Stopping, Mark turned.   "Don't come any closer," he warned.   "Why should I believe you? What did Tornick say in the tent?"

The boy took a few moments to catch his breath. "Tornick said you are not a friend of the spirit. You are not a good sign.   The spirit told him so. Tornick said he would send you out alone to bring back a fox. He said you would go home. Then everybody would know the spirit does not speak to you."

"Your people will fight if I go home?"

"Tornick will lead us against your village," replied Terigan. "My people do not want to fight. They want to live by the sea and have good hunting and fishing. They want to be friends with the Seal People."

Mark found that hard to believe. "If they came here to be friendly why did they steal my caribou?"

Terigan looked surprised. "Nobody stole your caribou. We skinned them and cut up the meat for you before it could freeze. I myself helped. There is so much meat we couldn't cover it with rocks. Some hunters are guarding to keep the wolves away till your people can take it home."

For a moment Mark stared, more puzzled than ever. "If you were our friends, you wouldn't let Tornick force you to fight."

"We do what the spirit tells us. Tornick says the spirit of wild foxes told him to fight the Seal People."

"Tornick lies about the spirit," said Mark. "He is the one who wants to fight. He lied to you about my feet. Now he's lying to make you go to war."

Terigan looked unhappy. "Nobody likes Tornick. He tells many lies. But no one can be sure when he tells the lie and when he tells the truth. He is the only one of us who can hear the voice of the spirit. We are the Fox People, and we have to obey the voice of the spirit or many bad things will happen to us."

"Fox People!" Mark exclaimed. But he knew at once it had to be true. It explained many things that had puzzled him. These people looked up to the spirit of wild foxes as a god and protector. "Let me see your charms," he said.

Terigan took out his charm bag and produced a small raven feather and an ivory carving of a fox exactly like the one Mark had found on the beach. Holding the fox up, Terigan said, "The best hunters of the Fox People have carved foxes like this."

Mark understood at last why Oka thought a fox charm would bring bad luck. It was the charm of the enemy tribe.

Three sharp reports of a rifle came from the north. There was a pause, then three more shots. They were signal shots from the village of Cape North, sounding an alarm to all the tribe's hunters and trappers.

"What is it?" asked Terigan.

178

"My people. They—they know I've been taken prisoner. Oka must have run home to tell them. Now they will be getting ready. They'll soon be coming to fight." He gave the bow back to the boy. "I have to stop them. I can if I run fast."

"But Tornick—" cried Terigan.

Mark hesitated. The boy was right. If he went home, Tornick would attack. If he didn't go home, fighting would break out when his people came for him.

"Do what Tornick said," suggested Terigan. "Bring him a fox. Then everybody will know you hear the voice of the spirit. They will say Tornick's dance medicine was not strong enough to keep the spirit away from you."

Mark's mouth went dry. "Why, I—I couldn't catch any fox but Kali. I—"

The boy watched him, waiting for him to go on. From the distance came the throbbing beats of a drum and the screeching and yelling of the mad witch doctor.

Blood rushed to Mark's face as he suddenly realized the truth. Terigan expected him to take Kali. He tightened his lips. He swallowed. In a voice that trembled he said, "If Tornick got his hands on Kali he'd be so mad he—he'd k-kill him. He'd kill

179

him and use some trick to prove it wasn't a real fox. Tornick is too smart for us.   It's no good.   It won't work."

Still the boy said nothing.   His dark eyes sharpened.   He kept watching and waiting, and his silence was harder to bear than anything he might have said.

Mark took a step back.   He had to fight for his breath.   He wanted to scream that he'd never, never give Kali to Tornick.   But he couldn't make a sound.

He passed his hand across his mouth.   His breath came in tight little jerks.   The drum, beating wilder and faster than ever, seemed to be hammering against his skull.

He was caught in a web of ancient Eskimo superstitions.   Words could not help him now.   Nothing he could say would stop Tornick from having his terrible revenge.   Many lives would be lost, many people would die before morning unless. . . .

With a sob tearing at his throat, Mark turned. And then suddenly he was running, running upstream, running around the great sweeping curves of the river toward his camp and his foxes.

16- flames and a scream

MOONLIGHT gleamed on the pebble ice like millions of sparkling jewels. Mark's shadow raced before him. Sometimes it ran at his side as he made the turns. Once he looked back for the boy

Terigan. But the young Eskimo was nowhere in sight.

His legs kept working as if they were no longer a part of him. His brain seemed like a frozen lump. It was as if he were running in his sleep, as if he no longer belonged to the world about him.

He ran on and on until it seemed as though he had been running forever. And all the while the mad beating of Tornick's drum pounded in his ears.

He paused at the gull cliffs, a mile below camp, to whistle for the foxes. Thin blue shadows lay under the cliffs of the shallow canyon. He hurried through and into the moonlight, and presently stopped to whistle again.

This time the foxes answered. Their yapping came shrill and clear, and much louder than he had expected. They could not be very far away. He dug for fish in a pocket beneath his parka. He was still digging when the foxes flashed over the rim of the tundra and came streaking down the embankment. Kali leaped against him, yipping for his reward.

Mark fed them. A dull sense of doom settled over him as he wondered if he would ever have a chance to feed them again.

182

That would depend on Tornick. Everything depended on Tornick. No one could be sure what he would do when Kali was brought to him. Tornick had lived most of his life planning and waiting for his day of revenge. Now that day had come. With tricks and lies he had held the Fox People in his power for many years. He was clever enough to fool them again, and to force them into a war they did not want. And if war came. . . .

Mark took a deep, trembling breath and sank to his knees to pick up his white fox. It looked so fresh and clean, so spotlessly white, that it seemed almost too beautiful to be real. The fox nuzzled him under the chin with its cold black nose, and looked up with soft liquid eyes.

Kali's trust brought a lump into Mark's throat. He felt like a traitor. Tenderly he lifted the fox in his arms and started back the way he had come.

He tried to tell himself Kali was in no real danger. Kali could not die. Caribou could die. Bears and wolves and birds could die. That was all right because there were so many on the tundra that a few less never made any difference. But there was only one Kali in the whole wide world. Without him the tundra would be a strange and empty place. Nothing would be the same.

183

Mark's eyes stung. The hard lump in his throat gave way to a sob—and suddenly the tears came in a hot, flooding rush.

Blindly he stumbled on. For a long time he walked and ran by turns, into the face of a rising wind. Angry clouds darkened half the sky. He was far below gull cliffs when he heard yelling and sounds of commotion. The sounds seemed to be coming from the left, where the Fox People had their tents. Tornick's drum had fallen silent. Suddenly he heard a scream—a scream so filled with horror that cold prickles shot up his back.

Though his legs wobbled under him, he made for the embankment. Blood pounded in his ears as he scrambled and clawed his way to the top.

He reached the tundra, and the first thing he saw was the fire. Less than a mile away black smoke and tongues of orange flame were rising against the sky beyond the jumble of rocks. The flames were leaping from the heart of the tent village.

Panic drove him on. Maybe he was too late. Maybe the war had already started. The wind took his breath away. Twice he stumbled and went down. But as he came closer he saw the flames die down. He could hear cries and shouts from the village.

184

Suddenly he tripped and fell heavily. Kali struggled to escape. Mark felt dizzy. The earth seemed to be tipping beneath him.

The wind storm swept in with sudden fury. It caught at him as he rose to his knees. Drifting snow drove into his face like sharp sand. The snow swirled and streamed and whipped over the ground about him, and in a few moments the whole tundra looked like a smoking wilderness.

Dimly he saw dark figures of men up ahead. They were racing toward him. Somehow he got to his feet and stumbled toward them.

Then Terigan and others were there, holding him up.

"Everything is all right," Terigan kept saying. "Tornick is gone. Tornick died in the fire."

"What happened?"

"I ran fast home," shouted Terigan above the wind. "I told the people you would soon be coming with a fox. They did not believe me. But when they heard you whistle for the foxes they knew it was true. They knew Tornick had failed. His drum dance had not pleased the spirit."

"Tornick had lied to us again," shouted the Eskimo at Mark's right. "Tornick was evil. He did not tell us the truth about what the spirit said.

185

Everyone knew he had made much trouble for us. The people ran to his tent with spears to drive him away. But Tornick danced like a crazy one. He tipped over the oil lamps and then everything in the tent was on fire."

Terigan said, "He never came out. Now he is dead. Now we will have peace. Everybody is happy."

17- into the white wind

WIND MOANED around the corners of the school building. So much had happened that Mark was still a little dazed. There had been the swift ride down the river by dog sled with all the Fox People following, their sleds loaded with the meat and hides of his caribou.

His friends at home had been expecting him, for a runner had been sent ahead with the news. There had been the wild rush of his family and friends to greet him, his mother's tears, people crowding and pushing to get close to him. Joe-Joe Henry and Pack Ice Charlie had lifted him to their shoulders and carried him into the schoolhouse.

Now he sat on the teacher's desk as though it were some kind of a throne. Kali was in his arms. His mother and father and Milly were beside him, and in front of him was a sea of friendly Eskimo faces.

The Fox People were telling of the day's happenings over and over again, as Eskimos liked to do. Each had something to say. Each seemed to think a miracle had taken place.

"Not in all the time that has gone before did man

ever hunt with the help of wild foxes," said one. "I myself saw it happen. The boy killed more caribou than there are fingers and toes on a man and a half, and all were the finest and fattest cows of the herd."

People spoke in hushed voices. Mark saw that his young friends were looking at him with wide eyes, as they had never looked at him before.

"The great spirit of wild foxes smiled on this boy," said another. "And now peace has come to the tundra at last."

Joe-Joe Henry, who was very proud of the fact that he read the Bible aloud every Sunday morning at the church meeting, cleared his throat loudly. "It is truly the work of the Lord," he said. "God does His work in mysterious ways."

Some of the Eskimo women blew their noses and wiped their eyes.

"We of the Fox People have come home at last to live by the sea. It is good. We shall be happy here."

Old Anga smiled and nodded. "You will need boats that can ride the big waves. We shall help you to build them. From this day your people will always be welcome at our school and our trading post."

Mark had not thought of the trading post. His

father would now be doing business with two tribes instead of one. He would have twice as much business. Everything was going to be just about perfect from now on. They wouldn't even need Texas Andy's little sending set, not unless his mother wanted to keep it handy in case of sickness.

Kali stirred and whined in his lap. The little fox was much too warm.

Then the moon-faced man came forward with Mark's hunting knife and knapsack. "Your rifle stands outside the door," he said with a smile. "You and your friends will always be free to hunt beyond the river on the hunting grounds of the Fox People."

"Let me go along when you hunt with the foxes," cried Terigan.

"Me, too!" yelled Oka. All the boys shouted for a chance to go.

Anga laughed. "We shall have to build our young hunters a large skin boat for crossing the river."

Papanick came up with his charm bag. "You have killed the first bear of the season and shot more caribou than all the hunters of the village put together. Now you are one of us." He hung his charm bag on Mark's neck. "It is right that you

189

should wear the best hunting charm of our village —the charm of the ivory seal!"

"A hunter needs dogs and a sled," said one of the Fox People, who looked enough like Terigan to be his father. "Tomorrow the boy will have his pick of our dogs, and a sled from the hand of our best sled maker."

There was so much noise then that the moon-faced one had to hold up his hands for silence. "Come!" he said. "Let the meat be unloaded from the sleds. Let the women go to their stoves and prepare the food while the men make ready the drum dance for the boy who has brought us peace."

"Yes, let the preparations begin," cried Anga. "There shall be a feast this night such as never was in all the time that has gone before."

People leaped to their feet and cheered. Milly and Tani jumped up and down, clapping their hands. Mark felt his father's arm tighten across his shoulders. He saw his mother's proud smile. But her lips trembled and there were tears in her eyes.

And suddenly Mark was all filled up with quivery feelings, and he felt like crying himself. But he didn't. There wasn't time. Kali was suffering from the heat. Kali needed his help.

In the confusion he tried to slip out unnoticed. But Oka caught up with him at the door. "Now I tell you the big reason so many did not like Kali at first," he said in English. "The old people say a fox in the village bring bad luck, because the fox is the charm of our enemy, the Fox People. But they were wrong. Kali and you bring us good luck."

"You helped," said Mark. "You were the one who made me go caribou hunting. And Terigan helped, too. I'm going to tell everybody all about it when we have the drum dance."

Oka looked pleased, but he said shyly, "We only talk about Kali now. Everybody like him now. Nobody ever set fox traps near the village again."

"Oh, they don't need to stop setting their traps," said Mark. "I'm not going to let Kali hang around here. He'd become a beggar. He'd dig into the garbage. He'd get so fat and lazy he wouldn't be good for anything."

"But what if Kali go out on the ice with the polar bears? Snow is coming down fast now. This is the time when foxes go out on the ice."

Mark hesitated. Somehow it no longer frightened him to think of Kali out on the frozen sea. Maybe that was where he belonged during the arctic winter. Only Kali could decide that. He was free. He had a right to do as he liked.

"If Kali goes out there," Mark said with a smile, "he'll learn all kinds of things. When he comes back, he'll know how to help us hunt seals and bears."

Oka brightened. "Maybe he teach us new ways to hunt."

Mark nodded and said, "I have to take Kali out of here now. He needs some cold air."

He went out with the fox. Heading into the flying snow, he made swiftly for the river.

Snowflakes stung his cheeks pleasantly. The wind tugged at him. He leaned into it and took the good cold air deep into his lungs.

Crossing the river, he climbed the far bank and stood for a moment pressing his face against the soft fur of the little fox. It came to him that having the love of something wild and free was far more exciting than having a tame house pet. It was a little like owning the tundra and the big sky and the clouds and the lonely wind, and sharing their mysteries and their secrets.

He set the fox down.

Kali ran a few steps and paused to look back. For a moment it was as if some wordless message passed between them. Then the fox ran on, into the night, into the lashing white wind that swept in from the sea, and was lost from sight.

192